THE MEDIUM OF BRANDEN BAY

KELLY MASON

Editor: Alison Knight

Cover Design by www.StunningBookCovers.com

This is a work of fiction. Names, characters, places and incidents are the product of the author's imagination or are used fictitiously, and any resemblance to actual persons living, or dead, business establishments, events or locales is entirely coincidental.

This book was written in the UK and edited in British English, where some spelling, grammar and word usage will be different to US English.

For Lottie <3

Hi, I hope you enjoy this book. If you fall in love with the characters and want to hear more from them, the good news is that this is the first in a series of books set in Branden Bay.

If you would like to know when future books in the series are released, feel free to sign up for my newsletter at:

www.kellymasonbooks.com

The current series is:

The Medium of Branden Bay

The Body in Branden Bay

The Haunting of Branden Bay

I'm Becky James, I was a city slicking millennial living and working in the financial district of London, until I inherited a huge Victorian house from my glamorous grandma, Constance. The house is set right on the front of Branden Bay, a traditional seaside resort in the south west of England. The bay consists of a yellow horseshoe of sand, sporting a posh hotel at one end and a traditional funfair at the other, with a pier jutting out to the sea. A wooded hill backs the town with a castle overlooking the popular tourist spot.

When Grandma died, I put the house up for sale, having no intention of moving as I had been living with Marcus, my boyfriend, in his Thameside apartment for the past three years. However, our relationship came to an abrupt end and as we worked for the same company, I decided it was time for a complete change. So I took Grandma's house off the market and moved to the other side of the country to start a new life.

Whilst I loved my new home by the sea, it was more than a tad spooky living there alone. I kept turning my head, thinking I saw a shadow moving around the rooms. I blamed tiredness; however, deep down, I was worried that I'd inherited more than just Grandma's house. Then one night, it got a whole lot worse.

I was having yet another restless night. It had taken me ages to drift off to sleep. Every time I relaxed for more than a few seconds, a jolt of static sped up my back. I snapped open my eyes as electricity fuzzed along my arms and pooled into my hands as pins and needles. I slowly lifted my head and squinted. *Is this for real?* A large dark figure sat on my bed wearing some sort of brimmed hat. I couldn't make out any features as it was a silhouette but my instinct told me it was a man. I felt my arms tremble. I knew he wasn't flesh and blood – for starters, he kept flickering on an off like a projection and at times I could see straight through him to the fireplace beyond.

Go away. You're not real – there's no such thing as ghosts, I said in my head. I didn't want to say it out loud, in case he answered back. This was more than some-thing lurking in the corner of my vision, this was a full-on ghost invading my bedroom.

But even though I could see him clearly, I was not

ready to entertain the idea that he was any sort of real. I crept across the large wooden bed on all fours. My knees dipped into the soft duvet. With teeth clenched and my hand in a fist, I thrust my arm into his chest. Pins and needles filled my fingers until with the third swipe the see-through figure disappeared. Gone. *See? Not real.* I brushed my hands together as if dusting off sand.

Taking a deep breath, I sighed loudly. *Am I going mad?* Licking my dry lips, I climbed off the bed. *A cup of tea solves most things*, that's what Grandma used to say. Grandma had never mentioned having ghosts in the house. She hadn't even read me spooky stories as a child. At bedtime we had tales about fairies and angels followed by a little prayer.

As I slipped my feet into fluffy slippers, I was sure I had nothing to worry about. It was probably hallucinations brought on by tiredness and too much sea air. I plucked my dressing gown from the back of the bedroom door and pulled it on. I looked around the bedroom with its plush red carpet, green walls and old-fashioned furniture. As nice as it was to have a room in keeping with the age of the property it did have an unfortunate 'haunted house' feel.

Heading down the ornate wooden staircase, I ran my hand along the smooth polished banister. The trip to the kitchen in the early hours was becoming a habit. I took deep breaths to calm myself. I'd been using relaxation techniques to help me with my insomnia after finding a book amongst the Mills and Boons on Grandma's bookshelf. *I'll concentrate on that,* I thought. The relaxation that was, not the Mills and Boons – after my breakup with Marcus, romance was way off my radar.

The grandfather clock struck a solitary gong from the hall, which reverberated up the stairs and around the house. *I really need to shift some of Grandma's antiques – starting with that clock.* Maybe that would de-spookify the place. But before I could remodel the house, I needed to find a job. I wasn't exactly dripping in cash. I'd noted from Grandma's old utility bills that I would need quite a decent wage to cover the monthly outgoings, which would be astronomical once winter set in.

I descended the final few stairs. They creaked with every step. I suppose you'd expect a house to sigh when it was well over one hundred years old. Reaching the kitchen door, I stopped short, staring into the moonlit room. He was there again, the same ghoulish figure, sitting at my kitchen table. Static filled my slippers and snaked its way up to my knees which began to shake. *I'm not standing for this.* I stamped my feet to eliminate the electric buzz and shut my eyes, whilst grabbing the door frame to steady myself.

Speaking slowly and clearly I said, "Leave. Me. Alone."

My voice echoed as it bounced off the kitchen floor tiles. Fumbling inside the doorway with my eyes still closed I found the switch and turned on the light. Peeking through slitted eyes, I saw nothing but the kitchen table and chairs. *No-one's here.* Sighing, I re-wrapped my dressing gown tightly around my waist. *I have to do something about this.*

FRESH FROM MY MORNING SHOWER, I pushed away any thoughts of shadows and ghosts. As I gazed out of my bedroom window at the sea view, the world appeared normal. That was how I wanted it to stay. *I'm sure it was just a dream.*

With the sun glinting on the sea, this was the first really warm day of the year. I decided to venture across the road and plonk Grandma's red-and-white striped deckchair right in the middle of the golden sands and read a good book. But first, I planned to pop to the shops and buy a picnic lunch to enjoy in the sunshine.

I sighed, nothing in my wardrobe seemed appro-priate for a sunny day in Branden Bay. Having spent most of my life at the office, much of my leisure time involved drinks and meals after work. So apart from two pairs of jeans and a couple of t-shirts, which I'd been wearing over and over again, all of my clothes were skirt and trouser suits. Marcus wasn't known for the fun-factor and we'd rarely ventured out at the weekend, unless it was for overtime. And whilst we'd been together for three years, we'd never been on holiday as a couple – not even a mini-break – unless you count the annual works conference in Birmingham. I shook my head, wondering why it had taken me so long to realise that I'd only ever been a member of staff to my boss-boyfriend, both at work and at home.

Shaking away the memories, I thought of Grandma's clothes, which I'd moved into the spare room. When I say spare room, I mean one of them because there were four bedrooms in the house and a large attic. I put my dressing gown on and went in search of something summery amongst Grandma's things.

Once inside the cluttered room, I looked at the rail of clothes in the corner. Grandma had been into everything designer. With her trademark sunglasses and flaming red hair she was often mistaken for being much younger than her years. Indeed, when together, most people assumed she was my mother. Luckily, we were the same size. I found a lightweight yellow summer blouse and teamed it with a cool orange skirt which just skimmed my knees. A far cry from the dark suits I wore in the city. After putting on the new outfit I glanced in the mirror, smiling and imagining it was Grandma staring back at me. Whenever I visited as an adult, she was forever dressing me up in her clothes, saying she loved me in the bright colours I would not have worn back home in London. I blinked away a tear, I knew Grandma would not want me to be sad, even if I did miss her so much it hurt. I wrapped a pashmina over my shoulders, picked up a pair of Grandma's large dark sunglasses and reached for a tote bag by her favourite designer.

I headed towards the front door and as I entered the porch, I saw a postcard lying on the floor. Bending down, I plucked it from the mat and turned it over to be met by the grins of my parents on the front. Mum and Dad were living the wild lives they felt they'd missed out on during their youth. They'd taken early retirement after selling off their legal firm and had gone travelling around the world for what was supposed to be one year but I hadn't seen them for two. They hadn't even come back for Grandma's funeral. I'd told them I'd handle it, after all they'd spent their whole lives looking after me and it wasn't as if Grandma would have minded. She'd have wanted them to carry on living their best life.

The writing on the rear of the card wished me happiness in my new home and explained that they were volunteering at a Borneo nature reserve. *We're holding an orphaned orangutang; we've named her Becky after you.*

Charming, I thought, *yes, I have red hair but it's not quite that shade.* I smiled at my parents faces looking tanned and much younger than they did during our tearful goodbye. I missed them terribly. However, they deserved an adventure. *I* popped the postcard in the letter rack and unlocked the front door. Stepping outside, I was instantly hit by the salty air which warmed my heart, reminding me of my carefree school holidays spent with Grandma whilst Mum and Dad were working.

I headed down my small pathway which ran alongside the front garden where there was a tiled patio and some ceramic pots that had once been full of plants. *Something else I need to do when I get a job.* I planned to fill the pots with colourful blooms – just as Grandma had. Once on Beach Road, I strolled parallel to the prom and wrapped my pashmina close around me. When the sea was coming in there was always a strong breeze.

I turned into Branden High Street, home to bars, restaurants and shops. I loved the atmosphere here. Visitors were strolling along, not barging past like I was used to in the City. Kids, excited to be at the beach for the day, were allowed treats from the touristy shops which spilled their goods onto the pavement with brightly coloured buckets, spades and nets. On the way to the store I passed the job centre. I stopped to glance in the window – just in case there was something that caught my eye. It was particularly quiet that morning so I decided to go in and enquire. *I'll have to get the ball rolling at some point,* I thought. I wasn't on holiday. I needed to find a new career. As I entered, a man looked up at me from his desk.

"Can I help?" he asked. He had short, cropped hair and wore a grey shirt, which I suspected used to be white. He had teamed it with a brown tie.

"I'm looking for a job," I said.

He gave a sarcastic sigh as he reached for a pair of reading glasses.

This is a good start.

"Take a seat." He pointed to the blue chair in front of the desk.

I swallowed, wondering if I could make an excuse and leave.

He tapped at his keyboard. "Name?"

I sat down. "Rebecca James."

"Address?"

"Beach House, Beach Road ..."

And it went on ... I tried to concentrate on the questions but was drawn to the way he flared his nostrils every time I gave an answer.

"Right," he said leaning back in his chair. "Have you searched our website?" He peered over his glasses at me.

No, I hadn't and I wished that I had because the in-shop experience was torture. I shook my head in reply.

He flared his nostrils yet again. "Firstly, I have to tell you that your desired salary is unrealistic. This is Branden Bay, not the City of London." His voice oozed sarcasm. "And whilst you're qualified to degree level, there isn't much call for Performing Arts around here, unless you wish to join the circus at the funfair." He tapped at his computer. "You may have better luck at Christmas, they're always on the lookout for elves at Santa's grotto."

What a waste of time.

"There's an office block in Alma Street, which houses the local financial sector firms and an accountancy practice. It might be worth sending your details there in case they are looking for a receptionist – as that is the only useful experience you have by the looks of it. But ..." He looked over his smeared spectacles. "As I said, your qualifications are lacking."

I rose from the chair. "Thank you so much for your time," I said, smiling away the expletives running through my mind. I guessed he enjoyed putting people down, so I didn't want him to realise he'd got to me.

Once outside I sighed and took deep breaths. What I was really upset about was that the guy had a point – I did have limited work experience. I'd worked as a receptionist for Mum and Dad when I was studying and then had started a temp job with the City accountants while I looked for acting work. The months turned into a year and then I moved in with Marcus. *My dreams forgotten.* The last thing I wanted, was to go back to office work. This was supposed to be a new start – a new town, a new home and a new me.

Continuing up the High Street, I stopped at the grocery store. The door dinged as I opened it and I noticed a woman dressed in red, staring at me. Her mouth dropped open. I gave her a quick smile as I picked up a wire basket and popped in a loaf of bread for sandwiches. I already had cake back home. Since moving to Branden, I'd got a taste for baking, having found Grandma's old recipe book.

I pushed my sunglasses on the top of my head and reached for a packet of finely ground almonds, I'd seen the call for them in a biscuit recipe. I walked over to the chiller cabinet in search of cheese. Hearing a voice behind me, I swung around.

"Hello there," said the glamorous woman in red. "I hope you don't mind me asking but are you related to Constance?"

"Yes, I'm her granddaughter. I've moved into Beach House."

The woman smiled; she was probably nearer my parents' age. "I thought it was Constance herself for a moment, before I remembered she was gone." She sighed. "You look so alike. I recognise you now, of course, from the funeral. I'm Wendy, by the way." She had dark, glossy, shoulder length hair and crimson lips.

I laughed. "I didn't have any summer clothes, so I raided Grandma's wardrobe. That might be why I look a lot like her today." I said, as I smoothed down the skirt with my free hand.

"It suits you. How I miss your grandmother." She placed a hand on her chest. "I remember you as the little girl who used to come here every summer."

I smiled. "Were you and Grandma close?" I only vaguely remembered Wendy from the funeral which had been like a blur to me.

"We mixed in the same circles and she was such a dear lady. I'm the President of Branden Bay's Ladies

Society. Constance used to judge our baking competitions."

"Really?"

"Having won Branden's bake-off for five years straight, she judged many local contests. But I guess you know all this."

"No, I didn't." I'd realised at Grandma's funeral that I knew little of her life that did not involve myself. If I'd known this, I would have asked the vicar to mention it. I felt suddenly like a very bad granddaughter and that I didn't know her as well as I should have. "She never spoke that much about herself, she was always so interested in what I was getting up to."

"Are you okay?"

I nodded. "Every day I think of something I wish I could ask her. I miss her."

Wendy put her hand on my arm. "Of course, you do, dear. It's only been a few months. The whole town misses her." She looked at the pack of ground almonds in my basket. "So, you're following in her footsteps?"

"I doubt I'll reach Grandma's standard of baking, but I'm working my way through her recipe book."

"Do you mind if I pop by and visit you? I could tell you some stories about Constance."

"Of course." I felt a warmth inside.

Wendy pulled a card out of her bag. "This is my number. Text me when you're free."

"Great, I'll bake us a cake."

"I do hope so. If you've inherited half of

Constance's talent, I'm sure your cakes will be delicious."

I walked back to the house with a smile on my face. This was the start of me becoming a true resident of Branden Bay. I only hoped that everyone I met would be as welcoming as Wendy.

CHAPTER 2

I decided that I would have to put my plans for an afternoon at the beach on hold. If I wanted to receive guests, I'd have to clear the back garden; it was a real eyesore.

I changed into my jeans and T-shirt and headed outside. I trudged through the long grass as dew left wet patches on the glitzy purple wellie boots that Grandma bought me when she was going through her music festival stage. She'd taken me to Glastonbury.

Wow, that's one week of my teenage years I won't ever forget. The memories made me smile.

I stood in the middle of the lawn with my hands on my hips, surveying the mammoth task before me. The garden had been relatively neat for weeks, but after a week of heavy rain, peppered with sunny spells, the lawn had gone absolutely bonkers and resembled a small meadow. I admit it looked pretty, with colourful wild flowers in blues, reds and yellows but it was completely unusable and nothing like the smooth lawn it had been, when it was fit for a game of croquet.

I heard a meow. Turning my head, I saw a ginger cat sitting on the roof of the shed. It had been in and out of the garden since I'd moved in, meowing at the back door and I'd thrown it the odd titbit. But I hadn't let it in – I didn't want to encourage it. Small, pretty and incredibly fluffy, with a clear presence – it was not like any cat I'd seen before. It stood up and held its nose in the air as it walked the length of the roof with a sashay any runway model would be proud of. After it jumped down, all I could see was the tip of its bushy tail as it wandered through the long grass towards the tree which had recently lost its blossom. I knew that tree would soon be full of plump Bramley apples perfect for pie. Beneath the tree was the wooden garden bench that I remember Grandma sitting on when the weather was nice. *That could do with a lick of paint as well.* The cat jumped onto the bench. I wanted to plonk myself down there too, but I had work to do.

As I yanked open the shed door, wood dust fluttered in the air. I put my head inside and a spider's web brushed my face. I wiped the sticky threads from my skin, waiting for my eyes to adjust to the dark interior. I shuddered, being reminded of the shadow lurking in the corners of my house and had a flashback to the ghost in my bedroom. *It was just a dream – get a grip.*

Spotting the shears, I plucked them from the hook they hung from.

I spent a good half hour chopping away at the tall grass, as if I was giving a giant a haircut. I needed to reduce the height before I could use Grandma's old push-and-pull lawnmower on it. As I reached the back of the garden, I heard a rustling over the wall. Someone was humming a tune in a high-pitched voice. I stopped and listened. The song was a nursery rhyme, a slightly out of tune rendition of *Incy Wincy Spider*. It wasn't a child singing – the vibrato voice sounded as if it belonged to a woman.

I'd seen people moving around at night inside the old prefab hut behind Grandma's house which used to belong to the Scouts. The singing stopped and I went back to my chopping, but jumped when I heard a voice.

"Hello there." A face appeared over the garden wall as a middle-aged woman parted the vines and peeked through like a jungle explorer. She had bushy, light grey hair and a huge smile.

"Hi," I said shielding my eyes from the mid-day sun.

The lady hoisted herself up higher, placing her arms over the vines. I guessed she was on a ladder. *No-one's that tall.*

"Sorry, I didn't mean to startle you, lovey. I'm Lynn. I wondered if you wanted to pop over for a cup of tea?"

Oh no, really? I realised that popping around would

involve a walk out of my front door then one hundred meters along the seafront, a trek up the High Street, with another one hundred meters along Castle Road to the hut. My hair was scraped back, I was already covered in grass, which was sticking to me as I was a tad clammy. *Do I really want to do this now?*

Lynn gestured around with her arms. "I've met most of the neighbours but haven't seen you about at all."

"I'm Becky," I said. "I moved here three weeks ago. I've been busy unpacking." I hoped that was a good enough excuse for not having made friends with the neighbours. It was true, I had been unsociable. But I wanted to get the house straight first. Sorting through Grandma's things was quite emotional and I'd needed to do that first – to get used to her not being there in the house where we'd spent so much time together.

"Have you moved in there alone, dear?"

"Yes," I said.

"I recognise you from the funeral. I did speak to you briefly."

"I'm sorry – there were so many people there." I'd gone back to London quite soon after the wake. I'd gone alone. Marcus – as per usual – had not been able to drag himself away from the office.

"So, are you going to pop in?" Lynn smiled at me. "There's a gate in the corner." She gestured to my left.

I remembered there was indeed a gate. "It's quite

overgrown," I said. It was hidden with the shiny green vines which covered the entire back wall.

"If you use the shears to clear your side, I'll finish mine and we can open the door when it's done."

I hacked away at the vines to create a gap where the gate sat. My arms jarred as I hit the occasional thick stem. I sneezed as the strong scent of cut vegetation reached my nose. But I soldiered on – I needed to integrate into the community and it was great that I'd met Wendy that morning and now was making friends with a neighbour. The thought of someone making me a cup of tea also sounded appealing.

I heard a heavy scrape as Lynn pulled open the gate. She stood in the doorway with a huge grin on her face. She wasn't as tall as I imagined, she stood at my eye level and I'm five foot two and a bit.

Lynn clapped her hands together. "Are you a tea or coffee? Milk? Sugar? I have herbal?"

"Tea, milk, no sugar, please." I pointed behind me. "I've a cake inside. I'll just wash my hands and fetch it."

"Marvellous," she said, clapping her hands even more enthusiastically.

Popping into the house, I quickly spritzed myself with deodorant, brushed down my jeans and pulled on my remaining clean t-shirt. I donned sunglasses and went to the kitchen to fetch the carrot cake. It was a masterpiece, with smooth frosting decorated with delicate marzipan which I had shaped into carrots; the way Grandma had shown me when I was a child.

Picking up the cake, a knife and two plates I returned to the hut.

As I walked through the cleared doorway, Lynn appeared holding two steaming mugs. "We'll have it out here on the bench."

I placed the plate in the middle of the wooden bench and took the mug of tea from her. I smelled the hot drink rising up. Salivating, I took the first sip. *Why does tea always taste so much better when someone else makes it?*

Lynn's eyes grew wide as she saw the cake. "Where did you get that?"

"I made it," I said cutting her a slice and passing it over.

She nodded as she bit into it and swallowed. "This is scrummy-licious."

"Thanks." I had to agree, it was moist, sweet and totally yummy and I'd soon polished off a whole slice.

"This is nice," said Lynn. "Have you made many friends?"

"Not really. I haven't been out a lot."

"Your grandmother was quite the lady about town, did a lot for charity. I thought the family had sold the house?"

"I took it off the market and decided to move here myself." I didn't want to go into the details with Lynn about my failed love life, so I didn't elaborate. I looked down as I felt something rub against my leg. It was the fluffy ginger cat and I leaned down and ruffled the fur on top of its head.

Lynn laughed. "What's your cat's name?"

"I've no idea. It's not mine."

"Cats often pick their humans. I think it's definitely a female, don't you?"

"I thought only male cats were ginger?" I said.

"Not at all," said Lynn picking up the cat. "They're not common but this one is definitely a beautiful girl." She glanced at me as she put the cat back on the floor. "You make a striking pair, both with red hair and green eyes."

I looked at the cat. "Grandma said our colouring came from her Irish grandparents."

"I don't doubt that. I assume you've inherited her gift?" Lynn placed her plate on the bench, having finished her slice of cake.

"She certainly had a talent," I said remembering the treats she used to make me as a child. Cakes, biscuits and puddings to die for. And from what Wendy had said in the grocery store, Grandma had been Branden Bay's bake-off queen. The cat jumped onto my lap and I placed my cup on the bench beside me. I was surprised how light she felt and realised that most of her size was due to her fluffy coat and that she was probably still a kitten. I stroked her back as her body vibrated with a purr.

"What would you call her if she was your cat?"

"She's petite, friendly and has a definite air of sophistication. I'd name her after Grandma."

"I think Constance suits her perfectly." Lynn stroked the cat's head. "Hello, Constance."

I frowned. It was never a good idea to name a stray cat. I picked up my mug and took a sip of tea. "How long have you been here?" I asked Lynn.

"We've had the hut for three months but have only been open for business, if you like, for about two weeks."

I turned and glanced at the hut. "What sort of business are you running?"

"A spiritualist church."

My eyes narrowed. *Spiritualist church?* Wasn't that the sort of place where they call up the dead? My mind flashed back to the night before. Constance pawed at my lap and I gently pushed her off. Feeling nauseous, I placed the mug back on the bench.

Lynn sat back and put her hands to her cheeks. "Oh, my goodness. I've upset you."

"I've come over dizzy. Probably overdone the gardening."

"Are you sure? You look really worried. That's why I wanted to meet all of the neighbours, to assure them that there isn't anything unnatural occurring here."

I looked over her shoulder to the old fire pit left by the Scouts. A picture flashed into my mind of Lynn dancing naked around flames with a recently slaughtered chicken. I gulped.

Lynn lowered her voice. "I know it seems an odd thing to do but spiritualism gives many people comfort. I thought with you inheriting Constance's gift you would have understood?"

I frowned wondering how a natural gift for baking would help me understand the so called 'other side'. I felt my heart thud. *Is this place the root of my problems?*

"If you have any questions, lovey, then fire away. I'm sure there's nothing you can ask me that your neighbours haven't."

Part of me wanted to leave but I needed to know more. I cleared my throat. "Is it possible for you to call up a ghost but it ends up in my house by mistake?"

Lynn smiled. "No."

"So, for instance, if I saw something in my house, it wouldn't have anything to do with you – would it?"

Lynn raised her eyebrows. "Did you call it up yourself?"

I shook my head. *As if I'd call up a ghost?* She'd referred to it so casually, as if it was ordering in pizza. I looked at the gate as I wracked my brain for an excuse to get back home. "It's probably my eyes playing tricks on me." I stood up.

"Wait, is it Constance? Your Grandmother?" Lynn looked up shielding her eyes from the sun.

"No. It's a man," I said as I felt the hairs stand up on the back of my neck.

Lynn stood up. "Well that must be quite unnerving

for a young woman living alone." She furrowed her brow. "We'll look into that for you, lovey."

"No need. It's probably my imagination."

"Let us come over and check. And if there's something there, we can move it on."

"Not necessary." I didn't want any ghost hunters in my house, *thank you very much*. "I have to go now. Keep the cake." I stood up and gave her a quick wave before walking through the gateway as quickly as my wellies allowed.

Back in my garden I shuddered as I walked up the lawn to the house. As I closed the back door I took a deep breath. I needed to calm down. My parents would be calling with their monthly update that evening, I didn't want to worry them. I decided to take a hot bath, relax and eradicate any thoughts of shadows and ghosts. I was sure I could combat this with positive thinking.

CHAPTER 3

"We have you on speaker, Rebecca," Mum said.

My eyes teared up at the sound of her voice. I was glad this wasn't a video call.

"How have you settled in poppet?" Dad said. "Found any work yet?"

"No. I'll probably commute to Bristol. I've looked on-line and there are temporary positions available there. I'll be signing up with a few agencies."

"I thought you wanted to do something different?" Mum asked.

"That's the long-term plan but I've got to get some money in." The thought of the twenty-mile commute didn't fill me with excitement but it was my best bet. "I've seen a couple of positions in the charity sector."

They chattered away about orangutangs. A lump

formed in my throat. "How long are you staying there for?"

"We're at the reserve for three months and then we'll be on our last leg of this trip. We're planning to come to you for Christmas – if you'll have us?"

"Of course, yes. I can't wait to see you guys." Tears fell down my cheeks.

Half an hour later, I stood in the kitchen making myself a cup of cocoa as I watched the rain bouncing off the back garden patio. There was a scraping noise coming from the door followed by a whimpering wail. I peered out of the window and saw a very bedraggled animal on the back step. *The cat.* I hesitated. *Don't do it, don't open the door*, I told myself as I unbolted it and turned the handle. As I peered down at the step, I caught the pitiful gaze of Constance – who was fluffy no more. Her wet fur looked three shades darker as it stuck to her small body in dripping clumps.

"Come in then," I said as she sloped in, her eyes peering out of a sopping fringe as she gave the faintest of meows.

THE RAIN HAD SUBSIDED to a gentle pitter patter, tapping on the bedroom window. Constance curled around my legs as I scratched her head, which now positively bouffant having regained its fluffiness, since I'd spent an hour drying her. I'd also fed her a salmon steak, which I had been saving for my tea the next day.

"I couldn't leave you outside all wet now, could I, Constance? You might have caught a chill," I said, pretending to myself that she hadn't moved in. She looked up at me, purring as I scratched under her chin. *How can I kick out a cat who shares a name with Grandma?* Having the cat with me somehow filled in the void left after Mum and Dad's call.

The grandfather clock struck ten, the sound seemed to distort out of tune as it travelled from the hallway. I gave a nervous glance around the room. The thought of paranormal activity going on at the end of the garden was freaking me out. Even though I'd watched my fair share of horror movies, with that being Marcus's favourite genre, it wasn't something I enjoyed.

I need to calm down. I leaned back in bed taking in deep breaths, just the way I'd learned to do through reading the relaxation book. As I tensed and released each muscle, I cleared my mind. Constance moved to the end of the bed making herself comfortable. It was good to have a companion to talk to and, even better, one who didn't talk back - *or leave the toilet seat up.* The window tipped and tapped less frequently as the rain ebbed and I felt my heartbeat slow to a similar beat. As my body sunk into the bed, I drifted off to sleep.

· · ·

I BOLTED AWAKE and stared at the ceiling. *Not again!* The house was still, my bed side clock told me it was midnight. I shivered and pulled the covers up to my shoulders. I turned to find Constance, alert and sitting upright, close to my head on the spare pillow. Her eyes were lit up and luminous green with her pupils in feline slits. She turned her head slowly and looked towards the window. I followed her gaze, noticing movement. *Oh, my days!* Sitting on the chaise lounge in the bay window was the ghost.

"You are joking," I said out loud, anger overtaking fear. I propped myself up on my elbows. Constance arched her back and hissed at the apparition.

"You can see it?" I asked her. *That's not good. Neither was talking to a cat but that was secondary to staring at a hat-wearing ghost in my bedroom.*

Constance didn't reply, of course, or even meow but continued to stare and hiss at the shadow.

The cat would not see the ghost if it only exists in my imagination. This was no hallucination. It was in that freakish moment that I admitted to myself, one hundred percent, that this stuff just got real.

"What do you want?" I heard myself say. *Don't talk to him.* I slapped a hand across my mouth.

Constance laid down flat on the bed, her rear-end lifted, moving from side to side as if preparing to pounce on prey. The light, which came from the street lamps outside, highlighted droplets of moisture on the inside of the sash windows. I saw the ghost raise his arm and he wrote a word on the inside of the windowpane.

A tingling sensation shot up my neck. I shut my eyes. "I need you to stop. Please go away." I reopened my eyes to see a word had been fully formed: 'Zoe' was written in the condensation. "I don't know who you are but I'm not Zoe. You have the wrong person." *I can't do this.* I shut my eyes. *Go away, go away.* I felt Constance rub against me and hiss. I opened my eyes and he was still there. "Look." I took a deep breath. "You need to go downstairs, out the backdoor, through the garden and there's this old gate at the end. That will take you to the spiritualist church. Ask for Lynn. She's really nice, you'll love her. She's the one you need to see. You've taken a wrong turn. Sorry, I can't be of any assistance."

I looked towards the window. The name Zoe distorted as it dripped down the glass. The ghost remained – a mass of shadowy dark silence. I thumped my fists on the bed. "Go away."

Constance flew off in the direction of the shadow then – poof, he disappeared. I blinked, staring at the chaise lounge with Constance sitting upon it, meowing. Everything else was quiet. A car drove past – the world was normal. *Was I dreaming?* The fading name written on the windowpane told me otherwise. *Static* tingled up my back as I let out a deep sigh and heaved myself out of bed.

Entering the kitchen with Constance by my side, I opened the back door and looked out to the hut beyond the wall. I saw a yellow light flickering as if a candle was burning. *They're in there now. It's probably them causing this.* I picked up a note, which Lynn had left on my side of the gate when she returned my plates. It had 'Call me' written on it and her number. I needed that woman and her church, to clear up their mess.

THE FOLLOWING MORNING, I woke with a sense of determination. I called Lynn and arranged to meet her that evening to discuss my concerns about their night-time seances and that I had, yet again, received an unwanted visitor. I'd followed this with a call to Wendy and invited her over for afternoon tea. I was also expecting the gardener I'd hired the previous day.

At midday I was in the snug, preparing for my visitor. The snug was what Grandma had called the second reception room, situated at the back of the house. It was a sitting room, much smaller than the lounge at the front of the property, which was huge and often had a constant stream of day-trippers traipsing past the window.

The snug had French doors which opened onto the garden. I had them shut at that moment because the gardeners were still out there doing what they described as a garden blitz. It had only been a couple of hours and the space had been transformed. Bushes had been cut back and the grass mowed. This was swallowing a large chunk of my funds but I was pleased seeing the garden regain some of its former glory.

I placed a café-style table and two chairs by the French windows. I looked out to the garden wall, upon which Constance sat, as if surveying the work of the gardeners. I smiled. Even though she was a cat, I felt as if she was looking out for me. The warm sweet aroma of spiced scones reached me from the kitchen.

TWO-THIRTY ARRIVED. Whilst I had only set out to serve savoury and sweet scones, I'd ended up preparing a full-on afternoon tea. Including finger sandwiches, a selection of cupcakes to accompany the fresh scones – all arranged on Grandma's cake stand. At that moment the idea came to me to hold a charity afternoon tea. That would be a great way to meet the neighbours and do a spot of networking. Maybe someone out there knew of a great job going. *So many people find jobs by word of mouth.*

The bell rang and I hurried to the front door.

"Welcome," I said to Wendy. "You're my first ever guest."

"I'm honoured," she said as she smiled and stepped through the door wearing a lilac shift dress. She looked around. "I haven't been in here for a while. Seems odd without Constance."

I sighed. "I doubt I'll ever think of this as anything other than her house. Come through." I led Wendy to the snug.

"This looks beautiful, Becky, and wow," Wendy said looking at the treats on the cake stand. "You shouldn't have gone to so much trouble."

"I've been looking for an excuse to get Grandma's Royal Doulton tea service out. Take a seat and I'll bring the pot in," I said as I went to the kitchen.

I smiled as I poured hot water into the tea pot. It was nice to receive a guest, especially one that was alive. I glanced through the window at the spiritualist hut over the back wall and wondered what the evening would bring. I pushed it out of my mind, I was going to enjoy my afternoon and worry about that later.

I re-entered the snug and Wendy raised her mobile phone. "Do you mind if I take a picture of you to put in the society's newsletter? I'm sure they'd love to see how Constance's granddaughter is settling in."

"Sure," I said smiling as I held the tea pot.

Wendy took a snap. "Perfect." She beamed. "I'd love you to join our group. We're a mixed bunch of all ages, although admittedly, not as young as you, my dear. But we're trying to attract a wider range of people." Wendy looked out of the open doors. "Your garden is adorable."

"It's just been cut back." I saw Constance approach the house.

"Is that your cat?"

I stood up and opened the French doors. "Well, I seem to have adopted her."

Constance sauntered in and sat next to me as I returned to the table. She stared at Wendy.

"What a sweet little thing," Wendy said.

I picked up the tea pot, swished it and poured out the steaming drink. "Do you take milk?"

"Just a splash, dear, and one sugar. What do you intend to do now you're in Branden Bay?"

"I'll be looking for a job soon. Not sure where to begin but thought I would start networking. I'm planning on inviting the neighbours here to a charity afternoon tea."

"That's a great idea, I can ask my ladies to support that. When are you thinking?"

"Not this coming Saturday, maybe the one after?"

"Have you met many of your neighbours?"

"I've spoken to the elderly couple next door and I've met the woman that runs the spiritualist church over the back."

Wendy frowned and looked concerned. "Are you into that scene, then?" she asked as she took a sip of tea.

"No, not at all. The whole thing gives me the creeps."

"I'd heard they'd moved in there. A few of the neighbours were displeased."

I was disturbed at how worried Wendy looked, considering my planned meeting with Lynn was in a few hours. I shuddered. "I'm not that comfortable with it either."

Constance started to meow.

"If I was you, my dear, I'd steer well clear. They often create trouble where there isn't any."

"Really?"

"Yes. What they do in their own homes is their business. But it's like some sort of weird cult if you ask me."

I wondered whether I should cancel my appointment. I certainly wasn't going to be dragged into their world. I felt Constance rub around my legs as if to calm me down. She must have sensed my anguish.

"Are you okay?" Wendy asked.

"Yes. I'm just not a fan of anything spooky."

As we tucked into the food, I felt a sense of impending doom.

CHAPTER 4

It was early evening and fifteen minutes before I was due at Lynn's hut. Rather than walk through the gate at the end of the garden, I decided to take the long way around to calm my nerves. As I walked along Beach Road, there were a few people strolling along the prom including a couple on bikes and a kiddie wobbling on roller skates as he held hands with his father. I loved the family feel of Branden Bay and at that moment I wished I had my own family there with me. Although it had been lovely having Wendy over for lunch, I longed to see a familiar face. I swallowed away my loneliness as I walked along the Victorian terrace which lined the seafront. The houses had been built from stone taken from the nearby quarry. A couple of the houses had shop fronts; one was a craft shop and another an ice cream parlour.

From the prom, I turned into Branden Bay High

Street. With the shops closed and only restaurants and bars open, it was a lot quieter than the bustling hub it was during the day. I heard mood music as I walked past Corelli's Italian wine bar and bistro. It would be nice to be able to go out now and again. I had popped into one of the pubs for lunch the previous week, but it wasn't the same as sharing a meal out with a friend. I felt positive after Wendy's visit, she'd talked at length about the ladies society and I was sure that she could encourage some of them to attend my charity tea. Maybe I should invite Wendy to go for lunch later in the week? I turned into Castle Road which ran parallel to the seafront. But as I neared the hut, I hesitated. *Should I carry on?* I heard Wendy's warning in my head. *"I'd steer well clear."* I took a deep breath as I approached.

Lynn stood on the threshold and pointed behind me. "You brought your cat then?"

I felt Constance curl around my legs and looked down. "Are you following me?"

"She's like your shadow."

I swallowed. I didn't want to think in terms of shadows at that moment.

Lynn stepped aside. "Come in, come in." She wore jeans with a floral caftan and a purple headband.

As I entered the hut, it was much bigger inside than I'd imagined. There were posters on the wall and a table at one end, which I guessed was some sort of altar. The place smelled of burning herbs. I shuddered;

it wasn't somewhere I would usually choose to visit but then I didn't normally have a hat-wearing ghost in my bedroom at night. I turned to my left and saw a young guy sitting at another table.

"This is Jeff. He's going to help me out."

I nodded at the guy who stared as if he was attempting to psychoanalyse me in one glance. Jeff was an odd name for someone so young. *Maybe he's early twenties?* He could easily have passed for a teenager. Having said that, the name suited him. He wore a Marvel T-shirt and looked very much like a bedroom-bound gamer. He had scruffy sandy hair, in urgent need of styling, and a failed attempt at a beard which was unruly and sprouted only from the bottom of his chin. He continued to gawp at me.

"Jeff," Lynn said in a stern voice.

"Oh, yeah. Hi." He pulled at his beard.

"Take a seat, lovey." Lynn gestured for me to sit down.

The set-up reminded me of a pop-up interrogation room, the sort I'd seen when watching old episodes of eighties police dramas with Grandma. The remaining tables and chairs were stacked against the far wall. I sat down on the offered plastic chair and opened my bag, taking out a plastic container I'd filled with cakes left over from Wendy's visit. I placed it on the Formica table-top and put my bag on the floor beside me. "I thought you might like some cake."

Constance jumped onto my lap, making herself

comfortable, as she kneaded my thighs with her paws. It felt comforting, even though it hurt a little with her having sharp claws.

Lynn made tea, chatting away about supermarkets and the advantages and disadvantages of the budget variety, clearly trying to put me at ease. It wasn't working; in fact it had the opposite effect. Jeff continued to stare at me. My palms became damp and I rubbed them on the side of my legs. The strength and determination I'd woken up with to get this matter sorted had evaporated throughout the day. *Please get on with it.*

Placing a notebook in front of her, Lynn picked up a pen, opened a blank page and smiled at me. "Now Becky, if you could talk me through your experiences, I'll note the details so Jeff and I can discuss them before we deal with any ghosts which may have attached themselves to you."

Will I need an Exorcism? This was sounding way out of my comfort zone. Wendy was right, I shouldn't have come. A vision of spinning heads and projectile puke came to mind. I prayed that the spinning head in my imagination would not become mine. The last thing I wanted was green ghoul gunk spattered all over my bedroom walls. Yes, I needed to redecorate but that was beside the point.

Deep breaths, I told myself. I needed to calm down, needed to get a grip, and I defo needed to stop turning to the movies for my paranormal facts.

"Jeff and I will investigate your place together. Jeff's

still in training but he has a lot of equipment. Sadly, his teacher Dave has had to retire under unfortunate circumstances."

I gulped, *what unfortunate circumstances?* I wondered whether he'd been possessed? Or found himself face to face with a human-eating clown? I was too scared to ask.

Lynn tapped my hand. "Don't look so worried lovey, these things are common."

It's not an infestation of fleas. "Really common?" I asked.

"Oh, yes. We're called to so many places in town to check out their activity. We've been to Millars Hotel, the fairground, and Emerson's ice cream parlour to name a few."

I made a mental note to avoid those places in future. Although Millars Hotel did an amazing cream tea and they had a spa. *Maybe I'll just avoid those places after dark.*

Jeff opened his *Captain America* emblazoned backpack. Lynn looked over at him and scowled as he took out his smart phone. She turned to me.

"So, when did the sightings begin?"

"About two weeks ago," I said, stroking Constance in an effort to calm myself down.

"What do you see during these experiences?"

"Shadows, mostly a man, sitting in different parts of the house."

"What does the man look like?"

"It's difficult to tell with him being pretty much a shadow, but he wears a hat."

Jeff tapped away on his phone.

"Does he remind you of any man you've ever known?"

I thought back to my ex-boyfriends. None wore a hat and as far as I knew, they were still alive. Well, I assumed they were. I'm not the type to stay in contact with an ex. Marcus would definitely not be getting a Christmas card. But no, the shadow didn't remind me of any of my ex-boyfriends. "I don't know that many dead men – he doesn't look like my grandfather," I said.

"If it's no-one you know, he could be a lost soul who needs help moving on. We can deal with that." Lynn snapped her notebook shut.

I jumped in my seat.

"Sorry, lovey," Lynn laughed. "Honestly, everything will be fine. No need to get spooked by a spook, that's my motto."

Jeff picked up his backpack to put his phone away.

Constance meowed and stuck her claws into my leg. The events of the previous night flashed into my head.

"It got worse yesterday. That's why I called."

"Oh?" said Lynn, opening her book again.

Jeff stopped zipping up his bag and retrieved his phone and leaned forward, as if watching a film that had just got to the interesting bit.

I took a deep breath. "He wrote a message on my window."

Lynn raised her eyebrows. "Go on."

"I woke up cold, to find him by the window writing the name 'Zoe' in the condensation."

Lynn blinked rapidly. "What?"

"Yes, like this." I put my hand up and drew out the word Zoe in the air in a dramatic fashion, making a slow squeaking noise for effect.

Constance jumped to the floor.

Jeff gasped.

Lynn stared at me and leaned back with her mouth wide open. I have to admit, that performing arts degree was paying off here. I felt rather smug, having clearly put the shivers up a couple of ghost hunters.

"What happened next?" Lynn asked breathlessly, leaning forward across the table and squeezing my arm. Her eyes had widened so I could see flecks of red in the whites of them.

My arm kind of hurt. Her grip was rather strong. "I told him, I'm not Zoe and begged him to go away. I even suggested he popped over here to see you. Then Constance flew at him and he disappeared."

Lynn released my arm, which I was pleased about. I rubbed it, now free from her vice-like hold. She scribbled away in her notebook with a frown on her face.

"It could well have been my over-active imagination," I said.

Jeff tapped away ten to the dozen on his phone

then stared at me intently playing with his scrappy beard. The sooner I got out of there, the better. I rubbed my arm. *I better not get a bruise.* It was short-sleeve weather and would show up on my pale skin.

"And that was it?" Lynn stared at me, her eyes still wide open.

"Yes. I went downstairs and saw lights on over here so assumed you had called him up and that he'd taken a wrong turn."

Lynn continued to stare. I glanced at Constance who was also looking up at me. And then at Jeff as he gawped in my direction.

"What's wrong?" I asked, looking at Lynn, Constance and then Jeff. "This is a spiritualist church, yeah? You see this sort of thing all the time?"

Lynn seemed to realise she was freaking me out because she smiled. But her eyes didn't. "Yes, yes of course, lovey." She stood up. "Nothing out of the ordinary. But there seems to be a lot of activity in your house and I'd hate for it to be anything to do with us. Now, I'm going to bring Jeff over to your place this evening and we'll get to the bottom of it."

"What, right now?" I asked.

"No time like the present. Is there somewhere you can go for an hour or two while we do our little investigation?"

I wasn't sure I liked the idea of giving two strangers – and weird ones at that – access to my home. Especially some sort of occult sect that I'd been warned about. And where was I going to go? The only place I could think of was maybe Wendy's. But I knew if I called her, she'd convince me to tell Lynn not to bother. Which I had to admit, would be the sensible thing to do. But it wasn't Wendy who was being woken up at night by weird goings on, it was me. And as alien as it seemed to have these odd people enter my house, I was desperate to get rid of the shadowy ghost that was making my life a misery. *On balance, it's worth the risk.* "I guess I could go to the pub?"

Lynn raised her eyebrows. "We can't have you going to a bar alone, lovey."

I was about to say, *I'd love to go to the bar for a stiff drink.* But I decided against it.

"I've a friend a few doors up. She's called Annie and is about your age. I'm sure she won't mind you sitting with her whilst we work," she said, looking a bit calmer. "Now, don't worry, Becky. I want to get this sorted for you as soon as possible."

Lynn went to the kitchen and I could hear her hushed tones on the phone asking this Annie to babysit me. I picked up the tub of cakes and offered it to Jeff. "Would you like another?"

"Thanks. They're much better than my mum makes."

It sounded to me like he definitely still lived at home. "So, how do you know Lynn?" I asked.

"I was having lessons with Dave before he ... er ...

THE MEDIUM OF BRANDEN BAY | 43

retired. I don't usually work with this lot. It's my first day."

Great, so I have a novice. "Have you studied this sort of thing for long?"

"No. But I've watched a lot on You Tube."

Oh, no. I rubbed my throat. *What am I doing?*

Constance sniffed Jeff's legs.

"I'm studying for a science degree at Bristol Uni," he said.

"It's interesting that you mix science with the paranormal."

He nodded. "I'm more into quantum physics. Looking at a masters, then a PHD."

Lynn returned to the room. "Annie's at home and would love to have you over."

"I'll take the cakes," I said as I collected the box then reached for my tote bag. As I picked it up, it was much heavier than I was expecting. As far as I was aware the only thing in there was my door key. "Oh," I said, seeing Constance curled up inside.

"Have you got your gear ready?" Lynn said to Jeff.

"It's in the van," he replied standing up and throwing his backpack over his shoulder.

What have I let myself in for? I wondered as I lifted the bag with Constance still inside and walked towards the door.

CHAPTER 5

I stared at the three-storey house with Lynn by my side. I felt the familiar furry stroke of Constance at my legs. "The cat's followed me again." I had taken her out of my bag and popped her through the back gate into my garden before we came, but she clearly had other ideas.

"Don't worry about that. Annie will love you both."

I hoped so, seeing as I didn't know how long it would take Lynn to clear away any spirits she found. I imagined telling my old work mates back in London about the situation. *They'd think I've gone loopy.* Not that they'd been in contact with me, apart from the odd email. *I guess it's out of sight, out of mind.*

Lynn pressed the intercom and the door buzzed as the lock released. I followed her in. Annie lived on the top floor of a house conversion and when we reached the apartment the door was already open, where she stood smiling.

"Welcome to the top of the world." Annie's blonde-tipped afro hair moved as she spoke. Her eyes were brown and friendly and she instantly made me feel relaxed. She gestured for us to follow her in. Constance ran ahead.

"Sorry about the cat," I said. "She's tagging along with me everywhere."

Annie looked down at Constance. "Such a cute kitty." She led us into an open plan living space with a huge bay-facing window, from which I could see the roof of my house and beyond to the sea, where a pinky-orange sun lit up the watery horizon. I placed the tub of cakes on Annie's dining table.

"I'll get the kettle on." Annie turned to Lynn. "Do you want a drink before you head off?"

"Not for me, lovey. The lad I'm working with today is waiting for me at the hut." She turned to me. "Jeff can be a little over-enthusiastic, so you'll have to excuse him but I'll keep him focussed on the job. If you let me have your key, I'll call you when we're done."

I fished it out of my pocket, *was this a sensible idea?* I hesitated. *Probably not.* But I handed the key over anyway. A feeling of dread settled into my stomach as I watched Lynn leave.

Annie poured water into an ornate tea pot. I smiled to myself, most people these days make tea with bags in a mug. This was something we had in common.

"I love your tea pot," I said.

"The best way to make it."

"I'm with you on that. Have you lived here long?" I asked, getting my question in quick so I didn't have to talk about myself.

"I've lived in town since I was five. Let's sit over here." Annie pointed to a long modern corner sofa in the seating area.

Once she'd made the tea, Annie sat back and curled her legs up beside her. She smiled widely and looked as though she didn't have a care in the world – unlike me with my furrowed brow. I opened the tub of cakes I'd brought and offered them to her. She took out a chocolate cupcake.

"I moved here with my mother from Martinique. But she passed away last year."

"Oh, no." I took a bite of a lemon muffin; it was comforting and I loved the zing of the zesty frosting.

Annie bit into her cupcake. "This is lush," she said and then finished her mouthful. "I've spoken to Mum through Lynn. It gives me a little comfort, knowing she's fine and waiting for me."

I bit my lip. "I'm not so sure I'd ask Lynn to do that for me." Annie was being really friendly but I wasn't sure I trusted her. *Is this how they sucked you in?* Being all nicey-nice, then wham, you're strapped to a table with some guy with a pronged fork about to initiate you into the clan in the most inappropriate way? I swallowed my cupcake too hard and started to choke. I reached for my tea.

"Did it go down the wrong way?" asked Annie.

I nodded as the coughing subsided. I put my cake down.

"You're lucky to have a gift I never get any contact from anyone," said Annie.

"A gift?" *Not this again.*

"For seeing the dead."

"I don't have that sort of ability."

"Okay," Annie said slowly with her eyebrows raised, as if she didn't believe me.

I wish I'd gone to the pub. I could do with a drink. I felt heat rising up my chest. These people were misguided as to what a gift really is. In my world a gift is something pleasant, ideally wrapped up in pretty paper with a bow. Like a new handbag or perfume. Not something which means you have to see scary shadows – that is definitely not a gift. More like a curse. I felt I should clarify the position.

"All that's happening at my place is that Lynn and her group have been calling up spirits in their hut and somehow one has got stuck in my house. It must have got lost." I gave a short, nervous laugh. I wanted to change the subject. "Where do you work?"

"Branden Bay Pier."

"That sounds interesting."

"Never a dull moment that's for sure," she laughed. "It's seasonal though. We only open at the weekends in the colder months. I usually travel to Bristol and work in retail in the winter."

"I've only ever worked in offices. I'm thinking of retraining." Although I knew what I really needed to do was to find paid work and quick. I looked out of the window. The light was fading. I yawned. *The interrupted nights are killing me.*

"If you get sleepy, feel free to use my spare room."

"Thanks." I knew that I'd not be falling asleep. I'd always viewed Branden Bay as a happy, cosy town but after these past couple of weeks, I was starting to regret my move here. I was seriously considering a return to London. I felt sick inside, thinking of Lynn and her scruffy, newbie assistant inside my home. I looked to the rug where Constance lay asleep – her life seemed so simple in comparison to mine and I envied that ball of fluff.

After an hour of watching a horror film, which did nothing to take my mind off events, my mobile rang. *Lynn calling.*

I answered it. "Hello?"

"We've found nothing here at all, lovey. We've had the equipment out and no spirits are showing up. Which is surprising, we'd expect to see something, what with the age of the house."

"That's a relief." I breathed out. Although this probably meant I was hallucinating. Maybe I dreamed about the cat seeing the ghost and diving across the room? I felt a little embarrassed for making such a fuss about nothing.

"Can you come back? I'll show you what we've been up to?"

I'd rather they leave so I can go to bed. Knowing the ghost was a figment of my imagination made me feel surprisingly sleepy. As if the adrenaline which had been pumping through my body during the past couple of weeks had been switched off.

"I'll come back." Ending the call, I turned to Annie. "They've found nothing. I'm so relieved. Thanks for babysitting me."

Annie stood up. "No worries, I've had a lovely evening. We'll have to meet up again some time."

Constance stretched in an arch on the rug, yawned and then jumped into my tote bag.

As soon as I reached the pavement, I felt as if I was going to get my life back on track. I carried Constance in the bag, with the empty cake box under my arm. "I should call you Princess Constance," I said laughing but she didn't even stir.

The prom lights twinkled in the darkness as a few couples walked along. I could hear the gentle swish of the sea as it lapped the shore and could taste the salty air. I breathed in deeply and smiled. The nearer I got to my home, the more relaxed I became, as if a blanket of calm enveloped me. Constance poked her head out of the bag and I lowered it to the ground. She jumped onto the wall and trotted along beside me.

Maybe the next day I would go out, buy a portion of chips and eat them whilst strolling along the prom. Followed by a soft vanilla ice cream with a chocolate flake atop. I wanted to embrace my new life at the seaside. To take my shoes off and walk barefoot on the sand, along the edge of the shoreline as small ripples of water lapped over my toes. I'd get myself a job – any job and focus my energy on doing the house up so that, come Christmas, I'd have a wonderful family celebration with my parents. That's what I needed – goals, and the short-term goal was the charity afternoon tea.

I took a deep breath, now confident that the ghost was a figment of my imagination. It was probably the shock of Grandma passing, then the split with Marcus and the move. It had all happened so quickly, no wonder I was seeing things. With that in mind, I clearly had to take control and focus on the future rather than letting my mind run away with itself. I nearly skipped the last few steps to the house. Constance sashayed ahead of me as I approached the front door. I knocked and the door opened.

"There you are." Lynn beamed at me

I waved at Jeff. "Hi again."

Jeff stood behind a tripod with some sort of camera on top. In his hand he held a grey plastic device. "Alright?" He looked down at the handheld contraption as it began to bleep. Lights flashed and the noise became higher in pitch. He looked up slowly, staring at me with his eyes opened wide. Lynn turned to him, looking down at the gadget which continued to flash in his hand. The bleeping noises escalated in pitch and volume like a video game. Jeff stepped back to study his camera and pointed it in my direction. Glancing up, I saw Lynn bring a hand to her mouth as she looked at the back of Jeff's camera.

Constance arched her back and paced the hall hissing.

I put my hands on my hips. "What's wrong?" The equipment started going mental and static shocks pulsed up my back. "Hey," I said. "That gear's emitting some electricity. Has it been health and safety checked?"

Jeff licked his lips then swore in the way a new guest really shouldn't.

Lynn slapped him. "Language, Jeffrey."

He shook his head. "This is insane."

Lynn moved towards me. "Come on, lovey. Let's sit down in your nice lounge." She glared at Jeff. "Turn that off."

He put his hand up. "But–"

"Now." Lynn took me by the arm, leading me into the front room.

What on earth is happening?

CHAPTER 6

The main lounge of the house was huge, with wooden polished floors, an ornate marble fireplace, two large traditional style leather sofas and a bookcase holding Grandma's reading collection with a stack of vinyl records on the bottom shelf, most of which were dated from the seventies. Lynn led me to one of the sofas and motioned for me to sit down. Constance sat to attention on the armrest next to me, puffing her chest out like a guard dog.

Lynn paced the room. "Sorry about Jeff."

"You were right about him getting carried away," I said. *He's got the makings of a mad scientist.* I stroked Constance's fur as she made herself comfortable on my lap.

Jeff appeared. Plopping himself on the opposite sofa, he stared at me. I raised my eyebrows at him and cleared my throat, adjusting my position. Quite frankly he had overstayed his welcome. They both had.

Lynn turned to Jeff. "Why don't you go to the kitchen and make Becky and me a nice cup of tea?"

"You're joking, right?" Jeff put his hands up. "At a monumental moment like this, you want me to make tea?"

"Now." Lynn addressed him as a kindergarten school teacher would their class, and Jeff scuttled out of the room. She turned to me. "Remind me, Becky, how long is it since you've started to see things around the house?"

I sighed. "Two weeks or so." I really wanted Lynn to leave. I had a strong need for sleep and visualised myself climbing the stairs and snuggling into bed. Having proved the ghost theory wrong, it appeared Lynn now wanted to psychoanalyse me. What other reason would she have for quizzing me on the hallucinations? Yes, it was nice that she was concerned about my mental state but I wanted to be alone. *Still*, I thought, *I should be polite*. After all, she'd taken time out to help me. A cool snake of static slipped up my neck and I rubbed it away.

"And is there anything you've done differently over the past few weeks?"

"Like what?"

"Calling out to your dearly missed grandma? Willing her to make contact?"

"No, absolutely not." I shuddered. "Of course, I wish she hadn't died. But I don't call her up. No disrespect, but I think it's wrong. I understand you've got a different opinion but I'm anti this medium-type, psychic-nonsense. I don't mean to sound unkind, Lynn. But it's not natural and is slightly freaky." *Whoops, there I go, stepping into the territory of being rude.* I yawned – my filter was definitely waning.

Lynn didn't flinch. In fact, she continued to smile even though I'd blatantly insulted her profession and everything she believed in.

"Anything else you've been doing?" she asked. "Have you been praying?"

"I might have prayed that the ghost went away but apart from that, no."

Constance jumped off my lap and padded across the room towards the bookcase. She looked so sophisticated and carefree, I made a mental note to be more like Constance. The ginger cat lifted up her paws on the book shelf. It was built into the recess next to the fireplace and she looked as if she was about to sharpen her claws on it. My eyes rested on a sky-blue book, just above her paws.

"I've been using relaxation techniques," I said staring at the blue book.

"I see."

"I read a great book of Grandma's." Standing up I walked over to the bookcase running my hands over the spines before pulling the book out. "Here it is,

Unleash the Calm by Walter Hill." I showed the book to Lynn.

Lynn crossed her arms smiling and put her head to one side. "How long have you been meditating?"

"About three weeks ..." Although it was just relaxation as far as I was concerned.

Lynn nodded. "That explains it, lovey."

"So you think the relaxation exercises have caused this?" I looked at the book. "It helps you get into a dream-like state of mind."

Lynn continued to bob her head up and down.

"So, I guess what's happening is that I'm connecting the dream world with my reality?"

"Hmm. Something like that."

"So I'm dreaming while I'm awake – creating hallucinations?" I felt as if I'd had one of those lightbulb moments. Like Sherlock Holmes or Miss Marple cracking a case. It was a great feeling. I gave myself a mental pat on the back. I'd always fancied myself as a bit of an amateur sleuth. "So I'm not seeing ghosts. I have an over-active imagination." I waved the book at Lynn as if it was an award I'd just won.

But Lynn had stopped nodding and was now shaking her head. "No dear, you're on the right lines but ..." She walked over to me. "When us mediums learn our craft, the way we link to the other world is to get into this dreamlike state you've referred to. It's how we connect."

I lowered my arm, staring at the book, then placed

it slowly on the mantlepiece and wiped my hand on my skirt as if it was contaminated. *That's going in the recycling.*

"Becky, I'm sure you realise that you're a natural medium and you've unwittingly opened the door."

Static buzzed in my hand. "No. I think you're mistaken." I took deep breaths as the buzz coursed up my arms. Constance stood a few paces away from me and bushed out her hair so much so, that she looked like a cross between a little tiger and a pompom.

"You're feeling it now aren't you? The energy. They're present. It's not the house." Lynn put her hand to her chest "It's not us." She pointed at me. "It's you."

Jeff walked in carrying two mugs. He stared at me then back at Lynn. "You've told her then?"

Lynn took one mug.

Jeff passed me the other. "You've got some power there, mate." He had an eagerness that made me feel like I was his latest college assignment.

"I'll see you back at the hut, Jeff. Wait for me and no gossiping." Lynn wagged her finger at him. "And take the equipment with you. I'm going to have a nice chat with Becky."

Jeff skulked off, clanking around with his gadgets, like a kid reluctantly packing away his toys at bedtime. With Jeff out of the room I felt calmer, even though Lynn had suggested I was some sort of medium. *That's total rubbish.* I felt that whoever's theory was right –

whether I was a medium or having some sort of wakeful dreaming – I had a plan to remedy it. *I'll knock the relaxation exercises on the head and everything will go back to normal.*

I took a sip of tea and pulled a face. Jeff had been heavy-handed with the sugar and I didn't take sugar. I placed the cup on the coffee table. *I think I'll try rigorous exercise instead. Get the endorphins pumping.* My brain was going ten to the dozen as I paced the room. But that was good, it was the opposite to meditation. I looked at the mantlepiece clock and yawned loudly, hoping Lynn would get the message.

"Do you want to talk about it?" asked Lynn.

"I'm going to stop the relaxation seeing as that's the cause of all this." I crossed my arms and leaned against the wall.

Lynn breathed in so deeply I could see the rise of her chest. "I'm afraid it's not going to be as simple as that. You've opened the door."

"So you say. I say that I'm dreaming whilst awake."

"Have you heard of Pandora's Box?"

"Of course," *I sighed loudly.* "Look, Lynn, it's kind of you to help and I do appreciate it, really I do. " I straightened up. "But I'm not a medium, I've gone my whole life not seeing any ghosts, spirits or whatever you want to call them. It's just wakeful dreaming. And I think you'll find there's not a shred of scientific evidence that this sort of thing exists. It's fine if you believe it – I'll not judge. But me? No – it's not real and I'm not interested. And I really need to go to bed." I walked towards the door.

"These things are usually inherited," said Lynn as she stood up and followed me.

"Well there you go – no one in my family sees the dead." I opened the front door.

"Constance did, and I thought you said you'd inherited her gift?"

"Grandma was not a medium and all I've inherited are her looks and a gift for baking."

"Constance wasn't one to come to church, but she used to do private readings when she lived here as a young woman, before she met your grandfather."

I shook my head. "She was employed to do fortune telling on the pier. It wasn't real. It's a form of entertainment, Lynn. You do know she was an actress, right?" I pulled a face.

Wendy was right, Lynn was trying to suck me into her cult. Next I'd be dressed in white and dragged over to the hut, Jeff was probably over there now, robing up. I needed to get this woman out of my house and quick. It had been a mistake to let her in.

"It's not going to stop, Becky. You need our help."

I put my hands on my hips. "I don't need any assistance."

"It's not only you that needs the help though, is it?"

I shut the door, not wanting the neighbours to hear

our conversation and furrowed my brow, wondering what on earth she was on about.

Lynn raised her eyebrows. "Zoe?"

For goodness sake. "It was a dream."

"It could be Zoe Palmer?"

"Zoe who?" Although ... the name rang a distant bell.

"Palmer. She went missing years ago."

That's where I've heard it. A teenage girl had disappeared. I remembered it because at the time she was the same age as me. She was sixteen when she went missing. Grandma had told me about it. But I was sure Lynn was jumping to conclusions. "There was no surname – just Zoe."

"If there's a chance it's her, you must help me connect."

I felt my shoulders droop. *This is ridiculous.* Constance rubbed against my legs.

Lynn gestured around the porch. "She needs to rest and move on and it has to be done properly."

I've had enough of this. I wanted Lynn out of the house. "I'm not a medium and I can't summon the dead."

Lynn walked up close.

I stepped back – I didn't want her grabbing my arm again.

"If things get worse, if you receive any contact from anyone called Zoe you must tell me about it."

"Okay," I lied, having no intention of discussing anything with Lynn again, spiritual or otherwise and I would employ someone to brick up the gate in the back garden.

LATER IN BED I left the lamp on and put the family film channel on the TV. I didn't want anything scary on my radar. What I really needed to do was to forget all of this nonsense. I'd had a rose-coloured view of a relaxed existence, living by the sea but my new life was turning into a nightmare, literally horror film stuff as far as I was concerned. A cult at the end of my garden? A ghostly, non-paying lodger?

I decided to focus my energy on the charity afternoon tea. Then, if I still had a ghost problem after that, I'd consider getting a regular vicar in to say a few prayers – and if that didn't work, I'd move.

I watched a film which reminded me of snuggling up to my mum on the sofa back in our London home. I felt tears spill down my cheeks and Constance rubbed her head against my hand and snuggled in close to me as I drifted into a restless sleep.

At some point in the night, I bolted awake. *Not again!* The TV fuzzed a snowy picture. Constance pawed at my shoulder, her pads were soft and her claws retracted. I massaged my neck which crunched as I moved my head from side to side and rubbed my eyes, which were blurry from sleep. The room had a yellowy hue from the dimmed bedside lamp. All I could hear was the white noise from the TV and the wonky tick-tock of the clock snaking up the stairs. The room had a chill, which I thought was odd – it was more like the ice of winter than spring. Seeing my breath in the air, I pulled the duvet up over my shoulders. My mouth felt dry. A ringing peeled in my ears, like it used to, after a long night of dancing in the London clubs. Boom – there he stood in front of the fireplace – the same figure.

I shut my eyes again. *I'm dreaming, I know I'm dreaming. This is just wakeful dreaming.* If I kept them closed and thought of something nice, I was sure he'd disappear. I thought of a pile of fruit scones with a thick spreading of butter, jam and a dollop of cream on top. Taking ten long, deep breaths, I slowly opened my eyes. But he was still there.

"What's wrong?" I asked him. I closed my eyes again taking deep breaths. *Don't talk to it, you'll only make it real.* I felt dizzy as if I'd just knocked back two shots of Tequila at a wild party. *What I wouldn't give for a wild night out.* Opening my eyes the room appeared to be on a slant, like I was in the crooked house at the seafront fair. Constance meowed in a low wail, the same way my old cat used to when he'd brought in a live mouse.

The ghost put a hand up to his eyes, looking left then right as if he was searching for something. He pointed at me. I grabbed Constance holding her to my chest like a teddy bear. I blinked and he disappeared.

"What does he want?" I asked Constance.

She meowed.

Am I going mad?

CHAPTER 7

*T*he next morning, I lay in bed plagued with memories of the night-time shadow. *I need to focus on other things.* I'd let Lynn's beliefs and opinion on the matter seep into my mind and place suggestions which I needed to forget. If I was to have any sort of normal life in Branden Bay, I had to eradicate the para-normal thoughts.

I jumped as I heard the doorbell ring. I hurried out of bed and looked out of the window; it was a delivery. After rushing down the stairs, I opened the door to find a large box. I'd ordered some equipment from one of the shopping channels during an insomnia slot. It included a shiny new mixer, a selection of pans in various sizes and three mixing bowls in pastel shades with matching coloured spoons.

Hmm. This has dented a big hole into my savings, I thought as I looked at the delivery slip. What with the gardener's bill, I'd already eaten into my dwindling pot of gold. I needed to find a new source of income and fast. I hoped the afternoon tea would indeed be a great networking opportunity. I went upstairs to wash and change.

An hour later, I headed towards the High Street to pick up baking ingredients, accompanied by Constance who was becoming clingier by the day. I decided to start every day with a gentle walk. On the way I passed the 'Save the Cats' charity shop and donated Grandma's *Unleash the Calm* relaxation book. I felt a whole lot happier with that paperback out of the house. As I left the shop, I breathed in the freshness of the morning and looked out into the sunny day. Constance popped her head out of my bag, sniffed the air and settled back down. I smiled and ruffled the top of her head; the normality of daytime gave me a feel-good factor. *One step at a time.* My phone dinged with a text and I pulled it out from beside Constance. It was Lynn, checking to see if I was okay. I didn't reply, I was not going to encourage any further dialogue with her.

I took a stroll to the grocery store, taking deep calming breaths of sea air, connecting to the real world. As I entered the shop, I noticed Annie picking up a baguette.

She smiled. "Becky, I'm glad I bumped into you. I'm having a get together at my place tonight, with a couple of my old college friends. Do you want to come along?

It's just food and a few drinks – not a massive party. There are only three of us and you'll make four."

I hesitated, I was going to invite Wendy over. But I knew I needed to meet others of my own age. *Although if Annie's tied up with Lynn...*

"Don't worry, they're not into spiritualism." Annie laughed as if she could read my mind.

I wasn't totally convinced but I heard myself saying, "I'd love to."

I PRESSED the intercom on Annie's building with my elbow. I held a warm chocolate fudge cake on an aluminium foil covered plate with one hand and my tote bag with a bottle of wine and a tub of vanilla ice-cream in the other. I felt a familiar fluffy body snake around my legs and looked down.

"Not you again. Go home," I said to Constance in a stern voice.

Annie's voice came through the intercom. "Hello? Becky is that you? Is someone bothering you?"

"Yes, it's me but the only thing bothering me is the cat. Sorry, but she's followed me here again."

Annie laughed. "That's okay. Bring her up."

"Are you sure?"

"Yes – she's cheeky but cute."

Climbing the two flights of stairs, I balanced the cake on my hand and held the tote bag over the crook of my arm, with Constance squeezed under the other. I didn't want her darting off into a corner somewhere. I heard Annie's laughter through the door to her apartment, which was already open. I walked in to find her giving a tall guy a hug.

He bent down and kissed her on the forehead then sniffed the air. "What's for dinner?"

"What about nice to see you, Annie? How are you Annie?" She pushed him playfully. "Always thinking with your stomach." Annie put her hands on her hips. "And be on your best behaviour we have an extra guest."

I stopped and smiled but they didn't notice me.

"Oh yeah? You got a new man?" He poked her.

So, this guy's not her boyfriend then? I thought. Not that I was remotely interested in a boyfriend and he certainly wasn't my type – way too macho.

"I wouldn't let you loose on any of my boyfriends – you always scare them off," Annie laughed. "Look what happened to the last one."

"He was a grifter."

"He pinched a pack of sweets when he was ten – not exactly a hardened criminal."

"Once a con always a con."

Annie laughed and noticed me standing there. "Hi." She pointed at me. "This is Becky."

The guy turned around and looked at me. His eyes were dark, darker than I'd ever seen, as if he was missing the iris's and merely had big black pupils.

Constance purred loudly in my arm.

"Hello," I said as I felt my face colour up. Clearly, I was hot from the heat of climbing the stairs, laden down with cake and cat. It so wasn't a blush.

Annie prodded him. "This is H. I'll apologise for him in advance."

H? He wasn't only missing colour from his eyes, he was missing the rest of his name. I heard a noise like a police siren and jumped and the cake wobbled on my hand.

It was H's phone ringing. "I'll just take this call – it's my mother." He went into Annie's bedroom.

"You look a bit overloaded there," Annie said.

"Yes. I ..."

I was interrupted by the buzz of the intercom. Constance jumped to the floor sashaying over to the rug in the lounge area and settled herself down as if she owned the place.

A tall woman entered. She was model-like. Gliding in like a swan she looked me up and down. I smiled as she lifted her hand in a royal wave.

"You must be Becky. I hear you're a new neighbour?" She smoothed down her blonde bob, opening her bright blue eyes wide. Now this woman had irises to die for.

"Yes," I said. "You can see my place from here." I nodded in the direction of the window. "It's the one with the green roof." Although why I said that was beyond me, with the fading light you couldn't tell what colour it was.

"What do you do?" asked Izzy.

Annie laughed. "Let Becky relax before you interrogate her."

Izzy called out to Annie as she walked over to the kitchen area. "I'm not interrogating. That's H's department."

H walked from the shadows of the bedroom. "Someone mention my name?"

Izzy smiled. "Talking about you darling, not to you."

H mock-punched Izzy on the arm. He turned and gave me a smile. I wished they would stop talking to me and let me take my coat off, because I was getting warmer by the minute. It wasn't even cold outside; I'd only put it on in case there was a chilly sea breeze when I walked home.

Annie put her hand out for the cake. "Ooh, it's warm."

"It's chocolate fudge. I've got ice cream in this bag," I said, pulling out the tub of vanilla.

Izzy walked back towards us and H put his arms around the shoulders of both Izzy and Annie. "I went to college with this pair. And for my sins I have to meet up with them every month for dinner."

Izzy slowly removed his arm from her shoulder as if it was a boa constrictor. "It's only a sin, darling, when we have to eat at your place."

H laughed in a deep rumble that I felt in my chest. "They aren't fans of my cooking. Doesn't help that Izzy here is a food critic for the local rag." He smiled in a very obvious tall-dark-and-handsome way.

I need to get this coat off. I hoped my hair covered enough of my face because when it flushed red, it clashed horribly with my locks. I wished I'd worn foundation. Since the move from London, I'd toned down my make-up, just using mascara, a touch of lip gloss and a bit of blush. Blush was certainly not needed on this occasion.

Izzy pouted. "It's not a local rag, we cover the whole county. It's the most respected paper in the South West."

"If you say so. Maybe you should move to the advertising department," H said, dodging a slap.

"I'll get us some drinks," said Annie.

Izzy followed her towards the kitchen area, leaving me with H.

He pointed to Constance cleaning herself on the rug. "Are you the local cat lady?"

"It seems so. It's not even my cat. Constance has adopted me and follows me everywhere."

Constance rose from the rug and trotted up to H, rubbing against his legs.

H smiled and bent down to stroke her. He looked up at me. "I'll stick your coat on Annie's bed for you, if you like?" He put his hand out.

At last. "Thanks." I removed my coat, becoming conscious of my little floral dress – another of Grandma's. I was feeling like the new girl turning up to a school-age party. All I had left to unload was the bottle of wine. I walked towards the kitchen counter and waved the bottle at Annie. "Shall I open this?"

Annie pointed to the fridge. "Put it in there, I've got one of those already open on the table. Help yourself."

After placing the bottle in the fridge, I filled one of the waiting glasses with a cool crisp white. H leaned against the table with a bottle of beer in his hand.

Annie waved a spatula. "I'll apologise in advance. The three of us can be a bit loud."

H laughed. "She's right about that."

I sipped my drink as I scanned the room. Izzy took a selfie with her full wine glass. Looking at the result she huffed and took another with a protruding pout.

Annie laughed. "Don't mind Izzy. She's the Insta-queen."

"The only 'Insta' I do is insta-porridge," said H.

I laughed in a squeaky giggle. *Where did that come from?* It surprised me more than anyone else. Giggling was something I never did.

It earned me a frosty stare from Insta-ice-queen. "Oh, very droll," she said.

H winked at me and mouthed, *we're only joking,* followed by a slow smile. I flushed hot again. I looked away and fluffed my hair forward to cover more of my face. *Is he flirting?* I pursed my lips. *He's so not my type. Don't bother, Mister Biceps.* Having worked in the City, I usually went for the suited and booted city type. Indeed, some of the guys I'd been out with, I'd never seen out of a suit. *I've certainly not seen any of them wear a tight t-shirt and,* I lowered my eyes, *those snug-fitting jeans.* Yeah, tall guys, good-looking guys but not this type of guy who was – *buff.* I realised I was staring at H's jeans and looked up to see him grinning at me. *Urgh, he probably thinks I fancy him.* Well he was wrong. *It takes more than a rocking physique to pique my interest.*

Annie raised her eyebrows. "Don't scare Becky off with your fighting. Look, she's gone all red."

Great, so I hadn't concealed the blush with my hair.

Izzy ran a finger across her perfect eyebrow. "We're winding each other up. It's banter, darling."

I felt an urge to go home, and hoped the night would get better. But unfortunately it didn't – it got worse.

CHAPTER 8

*A*fter a meal of yummy stew, I listened as they chatted about what they'd been up to over the past month, catching up as friends do. I thought how nice it was that they had a shared history but also felt a little left out. I wondered what my old friends were up to in London. Dora had emailed me that morning asking me to go back for a leaving do. But I didn't fancy it with Marcus there. Especially as Dora told me that he'd hooked up with the new receptionist. That just shows how little effort Marcus was prepared to put into a relationship. He couldn't even be bothered to look further than my old desk for someone new. I sighed, then realised I'd done so out loud.

H topped my glass up with wine. "Are we boring you, Becky?"

"Er, no sorry, I was sighing in ... satisfaction," I said

as I rubbed my middle section and nodded. "Lovely being cooked for."

"I hear from Annie that you two met through the spiritualist church?" said Izzy.

Great. I stared into my drink and felt as if all eyes were on me, *change the subject.* I looked up and smiled. "So – you all met at college?"

"Yeah, the fabulous four," Annie said laughing.

I looked at Annie, Izzy and then my eyes landed on H. Now, I'm not that great at mathematics but I counted three of them.

Annie waved her glass around. "We were all in the same tutor group."

H lifted his bottle. "Had our first drink together."

Annie laughed. "Had our first parties together."

Izzy looked at me down her nose. "Had our first wax together."

Was she looking at my top lip?

"Oi," said H. "I've never had anything waxed."

"That surprises me." *Oh no, did I say that out loud?*

"Why's that?" H asked as he sat back in his seat, his eyebrows raised but his eyes were smiling.

Yes, I did say it out loud. My face burned. I've always been told if you don't want to answer a question to throw another back. "So how come you got to hang out with the girl-gang at college?"

"My girlfriend used to be in the group as well." He looked down and took a slug of his beer. Annie and Izzy stared at him in silence.

Great, I'd obviously said something wrong here. Must have been a pretty bad break up. I felt very much the odd one out as they gave him one of those, *what on earth?* looks.

H broke the silence. "So, Becky, what's your line of work?"

I shifted in my seat. *Topic back to me then? But maybe this is a networking opportunity.* "I haven't been in town for long. I used to work in London on reception for an accountancy firm. But I'm looking for a new challenge. I'd like a total career change."

Annie stood up to clear the plates. "I went without a job for a while. It can be tough finding work around here. The only vacancies we have at the pier are minimum wage seasonal jobs that usually go to the students."

I looked to H. "What do you do for a job?" I guessed it was something manual with his build. I pictured him on a building site throwing a sledge hammer, bare chested with maybe a dusting of hair if he wasn't a waxer? I blinked away the picture. I seriously needed to stop visualising things, especially half-naked men and shadowy ghosts. Neither would do me any good.

"I'm a police officer."

"Really?" *I got that wrong, then.* "You don't look like a policeman" I said, picturing what he might look like in uniform.

The others laughed and my face really coloured up this time.

Annie gestured towards H. "He's the plain clothes variety. Detective Sergeant Blake."

"I'm just plain H when I'm off duty and I'm not a sergeant, although I'm prepping for the exams at the moment."

"What made you decide to become a police officer?" I asked. *Maybe that's a career for me?* Maybe I should be a detective. I'd played Miss Marple to fabulous reviews on the drama school stage. Although of course, Miss Marple wasn't a police officer. *Maybe I could be Cagney – or Lacey.* Grandma loved that show.

H opened his mouth then closed it again, failing to answer my question. I'd obviously put my foot in it again. I felt there was so much going on between this group of friends, things they were not prepared to share with me – the outsider. I guessed it would take time to penetrate this community. Branden Bay wasn't the London Square Mile, where friends were often in 'high-turnover' and hardly anyone had a shared history, commuting from far and wide to meet in the City.

Annie stood up. "I'll fetch the fudge cake. I've kept it warm in the oven. It's going to be amazing with the ice cream you brought."

H leaned forward. "I was at college doing a public services course. I planned to go into the Navy but my girlfriend went missing years ago. They never found her. After that I joined the force with some stupid notion that I'd be the one to find her."

Zoe. Picturing the writing on my window in my head, I heard a meow from Constance as she rubbed around my legs. I pursed my lips. My mind flashed a picture of the ghost, standing in my bedroom in a searching pose. Static shot up my back. I took a sip of wine – I say a sip but it was more of a gulp. I glanced over at Annie who was in the kitchen area, she looked over but avoided my gaze. *So that's why she invited me?* My hand flew to the back of my neck as the static worsened, like pin pricks on my skin. *I'm only here because they want me to help them find Zoe?* Constance jumped on my lap.

"Are you okay, Becky?" asked Izzy. "You've gone pale, like you've seen a ghost."

Oh, ha blooming ha, very cute, I thought as I pushed Constance off my lap. She gave a stroppy meow. "I'm just feeling a little dizzy."

Annie plonked the oozing warm cake in the middle of the table and frowned at H. She put her hand on my shoulder. "Would you like some water?"

"No, I'm fine," I said in a curt voice, reaching for my wine and finishing it off. *What I need to do,* I thought, *is get out of here.*

Annie cut the cake and passed it around. We helped ourselves to a scoop of ice cream. Everyone remained quiet as we ate. Although Izzy was not eating as such, she was dissecting the cake, lifting it up, sniffing, then nibbling it.

I groaned inside as I remembered she was a food critic.

"Did you use baking powder in this?" Izzy asked

"Yes," I replied. "I started with a brownie recipe which I adapted and added a little powder as I wanted it to rise."

"Hmm, I thought so," she said as she made a slight slapping sound with her lips.

"Oh, sorry if it's affected the taste." This was turning out to be a horrible evening. I chewed on a bit of cake. *Maybe I used a smidgen too much?*

"Don't take any notice of Izzy. It's bang on," said H. "Unlike me, she doesn't leave her job at the office."

"I was only pointing it out," said Izzy.

What an Insta-cow. I gave her a fake smile before turning to Annie. "Can I use the bathroom, please?"

Annie nodded. "Of course."

As I went to the bathroom, Constance followed me in. I could hear hushed whispers behind me, so opened the bathroom door slightly ajar with my ear to the crack.

"Why are you talking about Zoe?" Annie hissed, presumably to H.

I was right. I put my hand over my mouth to stop myself shouting at them.

"What's up with you, H?" I heard Izzy say.

I gently shut the bathroom door grimacing when I

heard it click close. *So, his missing girlfriend is Zoe Palmer.* Or was. I had a cold feeling inside that told me she was no longer alive. I shuddered. Lynn's nonsense about me being a medium was playing with my mind. This wasn't helping.

My heart raced, not with fear but with rage. One thing I hate is being used. Memories of Marcus taking me for a fool in London came flooding back. I stared at my reflection – my eyes seemed greener than ever. I bent down and stroked Constance, in an effort to calm myself down.

"We need an escape plan," I whispered to her. I smoothed my hair before flushing the toilet, then washed my hands to give the illusion that I had indeed used the facilities.

Returning to the living area, I slapped the breeziest smile on my face that I could muster.

Izzy looked up at me. "Are you feeling okay?"

Annie rose from her chair and approached me. "Is everything alright?"

I nodded. "Yes, I'm a little off-colour." I sounded like a right wimp but I had to make up an excuse, otherwise I would let rip and I didn't want any unpleasantness. "I think I'd better go."

Annie called out to H. "Can you walk Becky home?"

My face heated up again. "There's no need. I only live around the block."

H placed his beer bottle on the table. "Of course I can."

Annie fetched our coats. "Thanks for coming." She kissed me on the cheek.

Izzy waved at me regally. "Bye."

Constance was already waiting at the door, I opened it and walked through, followed by H who called out. "Don't drink all the booze."

I wrapped my coat around me as we walked down the road in silence, watching Constance trot ahead. If I was bothered about the guy, I'd have forced conversation but I'd run out of energy to make an effort. What I probably needed to do was sell up – get back to London and away from this madness. Get back to being who I really was – the city girl. I wasn't going to fit into this community, that was clear. As we passed the spiritualist's hut, the lights were on.

H broke the silence. "No offence, but the stuff that goes on in there is a made up load of er ... rubbish." He pointed to the spiritualist church.

I was surprised but just nodded.

"Some of the guys at work swear by them. Once in a blue moon they get a fact right, then everyone thinks they're for real."

He was right there. "I totally agree."

"Oh? I thought you met Annie through the church?"

"I only know Lynn who runs it because it backs

onto my garden. I haven't attended any of the meetings."

"I see." H smiled at me.

"I made it quite clear to Lynn that calling up the dead is plain wrong. It's certainly not for me. That's even if it is a thing. Personally, I think when you've gone, you've gone." I didn't really believe that but I needed to make it quite clear to H that I was not a medium or whatever Lynn and Annie had me down as. And most importantly, I wasn't going to be the one to find his lost girlfriend.

He nodded at the hut as we passed it. "I got stung by them. They convinced me they could find Zoe, my girlfriend, when she disappeared. Nothing came of it. Since then I've not given them the time of day."

We reached the sea front with Constance leading the way. At night, the stone walled prom was lit by Victorian street lamps and I paused. I loved this time of day in Branden. The resort had won awards for the most romantic promenade, which is probably why it was full of couples, hand in hand. It was a popular date-night attraction. But this wasn't a date. I continued on towards my home with H walking beside me in silence.

"My house is three doors up," I said as we approached my home.

"You live in one of the huge houses? On your own? I imagined you were in the modern apartment block."

He seemed surprised, but I guess a lot of people

don't expect someone like me to be living in such a grand house. Maybe it was ridiculous, maybe I needed to sell up. I pointed to it as we arrived. "I told you my house backed on to the spiritualist hut. Here we are."

Constance jumped on the wall and hissed, staring up at the house.

"Your cat seems to have seen something it doesn't like," said H.

I paused and looked up to the top floor. I was sure I saw something move. *Oh no, not the shadow again?*

H placed a hand on my arm. "Are you okay?"

A tingle shot up from where his hand was. "It's probably my eyes playing tricks on me but I thought I saw something upstairs."

"What? In your house?"

"Yes in the bedroom on the first floor at the front."

His body stiffened as if going into Action Man pose. I have to say I was kind of impressed. I imagined him spinning around and then in a blink of an eye he'd be dressed in Lycra with a cape flapping in the sea breeze. He did, in truth, have a super-hero-esque physique

My eyes came back into focus and he was frowning at me as I remembered we were discussing the serious subject of a possible intruder. His expression was dark.

I swallowed. "It was probably just my hair," I said, tucking it behind my ears. "Maybe it blew across my face?"

"I'll come in and check. To be on the safe side," he said as I took out my key and unlocked the door.

CHAPTER 9

I hadn't planned to invite H in for coffee but perhaps it was sensible, under the circumstances with there being a possible intruder. After all he was a bona-fide detective.

Once inside the house, it seemed quiet. I turned the lights on and they flickered.

"You might want to get someone to look at your electrics," H whispered as if not wanting to disturb an intruder. "They could need modernising."

"Yes probably, I'm forever getting static running up my body," I whispered back.

H inspected the control board visible in the porch. "The whole house probably needs rewiring," he said in a low voice. "Although the box looks modern."

I removed my coat.

"I'll check down here first." He put a finger to his lips, as if to say *shush* and left me in the porch.

Constance snaked around the inner door and I watched her climb the stairs.

H soon returned. "Nothing down here. I'll check upstairs."

"The first door on the right is where I've piled my late grandma's stuff so mind you don't trip over anything."

I turned and looked in my letter rack and flicked through the junk mail. After a minute or so I felt someone tap me on the back.

I yelped. "Aghh!" and put my hand to my chest.

"It really did make you nervous, didn't it?" said H.

"Sorry, I'm so jumpy these days."

"The only thing upstairs was your cat. You might have a mouse up there though as she was hissing at the wardrobe but I checked and there was no-one inside."

"I see," I said remembering Constance hissing at the shadow. *So he's back.*

"How do you cope living in a big old house on your own?"

I pushed my hair behind my ears. "I'm used to the house; I visited my grandma every year since I was five. Although it's the first time I've lived here alone. Would you like a hot drink?" I thought I should offer. After all, he had checked the house – it wasn't like inviting him in for coffee. I'd never have invited him in socially. It was totally due to there being a potential emergency situation.

"Yeah, black coffee would be great." He glanced through the front lounge door as we passed it.

I overtook him. "I've loads of cake. Do you want some?" I called over my shoulder.

"I'm not sure I can manage another after that chocolate one, which I have to say was perfect, regardless of what Izzy said." He followed me towards the kitchen.

Opening the back door, we took our drinks outside. H changed his mind about eating and chose a sultana scone which we shared, half each with butter and jam.

"Moving to a new town must be hard," he said before taking a bite.

I nodded. "I need to integrate myself more."

"Well you went down well with our gang. Trust me you'd know if they didn't like you." He laughed, pointing towards Annie's apartment.

I could see Annie and Izzy moving around inside. "I think they're dancing."

"I think they've drunk all the booze," he said.

"You're missing out."

H shook his head. "To be honest I wasn't in the mood for it this evening. Had a tough day at work."

"I guess it's one of those jobs that's difficult to turn off from." Whilst I wasn't remotely interested in anything romantic, I was genuinely intrigued about his line of work.

"True, my mind rattles on. Some drown themselves

in drink, some go to church and others meditate. None of those things appeal to me."

I placed my cup on the wall. "Do you know what? I tried something like meditation recently but it was some heavy stuff and I started seeing things."

"Best to avoid anything like that. That's my advice."

I nodded. "I thought I was going crazy." It was nice to have a sensible conversation. "I've found exercise helps clear my mind."

"Are you a member of the gym?"

"No not yet." *Or ever.* I didn't want to tell him that my exercise regime amounted to a morning stroll up the High Street to the shops to buy baking ingredients. Although I noticed I was starting to fill out slightly, which I wasn't too unhappy about - I've always been stick thin. At school I had been taunted for it. They called me a ginger stick insect. People often assume that if you're skinny you work out. Not so in my case.

"I'm a member of the gym if you want to come one morning as my guest, try it out before you sign up?" said H.

Now I had gone and done it. "I just go for a morning run." *Maybe a slight exaggeration.*

"Great, I'll meet you the day after tomorrow. Seven a.m?"

"Yeah, sure." *Why on earth did I agree to that?*

H drained his cup. "I better get off then. Early start tomorrow."

As I watched him walk to the door, I decided to text

him the following day to cancel. It wasn't until he was out of shouting distance that I realised, I didn't have his number.

THE FOLLOWING MORNING, I'd calmed down after the dinner party. I shouldn't have taken it so personally. Let's face it, if one of my friends had gone missing and I thought there was some way of finding out what happened to her, I'd probably have pursued it too. If I was going to integrate myself into Branden Bay, I needed to build bridges not burn them – especially with the charity afternoon tea looming up. I had to face facts; the ghost wasn't going anywhere – I'd seen him out of the corner of my eye when I'd gone to bed. It was as if he was saying *Don't forget about me.* I hoped that if I ignored him, he would realise that I was not the one to help him and he'd move on to someone else. All I wanted to concentrate on for now was the afternoon tea and networking to find myself a new career. With that in mind, I texted Annie and invited her to meet me for lunch in the Branden Arms.

At twelve thirty I walked along Beach Road towards the pub with Constance at heel. It was situated halfway between my house and the pier. Once I reached the door, I looked down to find Constance was still with me, so I lowered my bag and she hopped inside. The aroma of beer and food hit me as soon as I walked in. It was a traditional British pub with a dark wooden bar and matching old tables already filling up with customers. Annie waved to me from a booth.

"Do you want a drink?" I asked as I reached the table.

"I've got a bottle and already have a glass for you. I'm only working half day today as I've got a guy coming over to service the boiler this afternoon."

I sat down in the booth and placed the bag at the end and Constance poked her fluffy head out.

Annie laughed. "I know you said the cat goes everywhere with you but I didn't realise that included the pub."

"Tell me about it," I said as Constance jumped out of the bag and sat next to me. I smiled, every time I looked at her I felt a warmth inside. I stroked her and she leaned into me purring. I turned back to Annie. "I wanted to get your opinion on an afternoon tea I'm arranging."

"At your house?"

"Yes. I'm planning on doing a charity event to raise money for the local hospice which helped out with Grandma."

"That's a brilliant idea," said Annie. "I'm sure you'll raise loads, I can't wait."

I felt a flutter of excitement as I took a sip of wine. "I'm going to swap some of Grandma's old antiques for crockery at the charity shop. But I do need to find some tables and chairs."

Annie refilled her glass. "If Lynn is around when I

pass the hut on my way home, do you want me to ask about a loan of hers? She has a stack of them."

I hesitated and bit my lip, remembering the pile of tables I'd seen at the hut. With cloths over them they would be ideal. Constance pawed my arm. "Okay," I said. As much as I didn't want to see Lynn again, the tables would be of great help. I took a deep breath. I had to tackle the Zoe subject and talk of the hut had probably brought it to Annie's mind.

"Sorry about last night," I said. "You know, coming over weird and wanting to go home."

"Hey, no worries. I realise we're a bit loud."

I nodded. "It wasn't that, though." I moved around in my seat. *May as well get straight to the point.*

Constance put a paw on my hand.

"It was when H mentioned Zoe. I thought you'd only invited me over because you thought I had a message from her. You know, from the other side. I overheard you talking about her when I went to the bathroom."

"Oh," said Annie, rubbing her forehead with the tips of her fingers.

"I need to clarify with you, honestly, I'm not able to summon ghosts or anything. I'm scared witless by the whole thing and I've no idea how to talk to the dead. I just dreamed about a man and saw the name Zoe. That's all." Maybe I was playing it down but that was what was needed.

"It's all my fault." Annie frowned. "I was so

surprised H mentioned her, he never ever talks about Zoe. Lynn told me about it before I met you. I warned Izzy, before she came over, not to mention Zoe in case you thought that's why I'd invited you over. But as H never talks about her, he didn't get the memo." Annie gave a short laugh. "I'm so sorry. I invited you over because you're great company."

"I don't know about that," I said.

Annie took a sip of her drink and lowered her voice. "People around here got obsessed with the whole Zoe story – it's become an unsolved local legend."

"Sounds like an awful time."

"Yes, and we fell out for a while. There was a lot of tension between H and Izzy."

"Really?"

"Just the usual teen jealousy. But these things tend to get blown out of proportion under that sort of pressure."

So Izzy was jealous of Zoe and H?

"Zoe and Izzy had an awful bust up just before she went missing. Poor Izzy, she never got to say sorry." Annie sat up straight and smiled. "So, do you know who to invite to this afternoon tea?"

"I'm planning on delivering leaflets to the neighbouring streets. I have a contact at the Branden Bay Ladies' Society." I was sure Wendy would be able to drum up a lot of business.

"I'll ask Lynn for some suggestions for you. She

knows who's who in the community." Annie picked up the menu. "All this talk is making me hungry. Shall we order?"

I nodded. "I'll get the food. I think I'll go for ham, egg and chips."

"Make that two." Annie moved close and spoke in a low voice. "I'd better warn you before you go up there. There's a young guy at the bar who can't take his eyes off you."

I raised my eyebrows. "Really?"

"Yes, he's at three o'clock and I think he may be in love."

I glanced over. *Great.* I saw Jeff leaning up against the bar staring at me.

"He's gazing at you like you're an angel or something," said Annie.

I bit my lip. *I think he thinks I am.* "I'll order our meals." I made a note of the table number and checked to make sure Constance did not follow me. I headed to the bar. There was no point ignoring Jeff, I could tell by the look in his eye he would approach me, anyway. At least if I went to him it would be a private conversation.

Jeff put his pint of cola on the bar and stood up straight pushing his chest out. "Hi, Becky. I thought it was you. How are you? Have you got rid of your paranormal activity?"

I sighed. "Didn't Lynn update you?"

"No, she sent me home." Jeff stroked his scrappy beard. "She didn't help you shift it?"

I shook my head. "Lynn seems interested in developing what she sees as my gift but I just want the ghost to move on." I wondered why I was being so honest with him. He seemed harmless, I guess, like a kid brother.

Jeff blinked and rubbed his hands. "I could help. The service I'm developing includes getting rid. And I could have done that for you too if Lynn hadn't thrown me out like that. But maybe she has other motives."

"Like what?"

"I asked Mum about the Zoe mystery last night. She says Lynn had a thing with Zoe's dad."

"A thing?"

"That's what she said." He took a sip of his cola. "I can do a clean-up for you. I charge though. The equipment wasn't cheap and I bought a lot of it on a credit card and Mum opened my statement and went mad, so I'm after paying it back quick."

"Okay, I understand." *Seems fair enough.*

He took his phone out of his pocket. "Give me your number and I'll text you mine. Have a think about it and let me know."

I read out my number and he plugged it into his phone.

"But Lynn said there's nothing in my house, that it's all me."

He nodded. "We'll get that ghost of yours across the bridge then ask him to stop bothering you and to never come back."

I felt a buzzing up my neck. Jeff made it all sound so simple.

"Although, your gift is insane. If you did want to develop it and combine your powers with my equipment, we could go places." He waggled his faint eyebrows at me. "I'm talking world-renowned. I'm talking TV – reality TV."

Is this guy for real? "I have to put in my lunch order – but I'll let you know."

Annie grinned as I reached the table. "He's a quick mover then, exchanging numbers like that."

"It's Jeff – the guy who went to my house with Lynn and his equipment looking for paranormal activity."

Annie looked over to the bar. "He looks like he should be in Scooby Doo."

I laughed. "I knew he reminded me of someone."

"What did he want?"

Constance meowed and stared at me, then at Jeff. I stroked her and pulled her close, not wanting her to be spotted by the bar staff. I wasn't sure if pets were allowed.

"Come on, spill." Annie's eyes opened wide.

I wasn't about to tell Annie I was considering Jeff's services in case she told Lynn. "He said we could go places together as ghost hunters. Make it big on TV."

Annie laughed. "You said you wanted a career change."

I looked back at Jeff finishing off his drink at the bar. If he was right about Lynn and she did have a vested interest in the Zoe situation, I guessed she was unlikely to leave me alone while the ghost was still in contact. I decided I would definitely get Jeff around to zap the shadow. After all, the ghost would surely just move on to someone else who would be much better suited at conversing with the dead than me.

CHAPTER 10

As I pulled a tray full of sweet-smelling chocolate brownie out of the oven, I heard the doorbell ring and glanced at the kitchen clock. *Eight o'clock already?* It was Jeff, I'd texted him after lunch and invited him over. I'd become so engrossed in my baking that I had forgotten the time. I placed the tray on my wooden chopping block and removed my oven gloves before heading to the front of the house.

As I opened the door I was met with Jeff's eager gaze. "I'm ready to get rid of your ghosts," he said.

"Shhh," I said, looking at his van parked outside with *Paranormal Jeff,* emblazoned on the side panel.

"Do you like my new sign? I had it delivered today. It's magnetic so I can take it on and off," he said in a loud voice. "Mum isn't too keen on the paranormal stuff. I told her I'd given it up because she was convinced I'd joined the occult." He laughed loudly.

"Do you think it's a good idea then? Maybe you should take it off now?"

"It's great for advertising," he said.

I pulled him in, hoping the neighbours did not notice the sign on the van. It might be great for promoting his business but could put them off my charity event. Hopefully the neighbours would assume that *Paranormal Jeff* was parked up for a stroll along the prom, rather than a guest in my house.

Jeff gestured toward the inside of the now closed door. "The gear's in the van."

"We'll get it in a little while," I said. *When it's dark.*

Once inside the front room, I pulled the blinds and turned the lights on. "Look Jeff, I hope you've not told anyone about this."

"Of course not. I don't want Lynn to know do I? She'd go mad." Jeff paused, "And I haven't told Mum." Jeff looked down. "Mum says to stay away from you. She says the whole Zoe business was a sorry state of affairs and to leave it well alone." He looked at me. "She says you spell trouble."

I was getting a clear picture of Jeff's homelife as I left him in the lounge nosing through my bookcase. I put the kettle on and cut the pan of chocolate brownie into eight slices and moved them to cool having placed two warm and oozing portions on plates. *I hope he's not staying the night.* I wasn't quite sure of the process. *I wish I'd gone over the plan in detail before he arrived.* I looked out of the kitchen window towards the hut and pulled down the blind. Constance gave an angry meow from the kitchen doorway. She arched her back as I felt static travel up my neck and my heartbeat quickened. I shuddered. When Constance was unsettled it gave me the jitters.

I entered the lounge with a tray of refreshments and placed them on the coffee table.

Jeff had one of Grandma's old 70's vinyl albums in his hand.

"Your collection is insane." Placing it back on the shelf he turned back to me. "It'll be one hundred pounds, which is 'mate's rates'. The usual charge is double that," he said as he held out his hand.

"You want cash?"

Jeff frowned and fished his phone out of his pocket. "Okay, if you haven't got it, here are my bank details." He showed me the screen.

I tapped his details into my banking app.

"It could be a long night," he said.

I really hope not, I thought as I verified the transaction.

"Do you want me to run through everything with you first, so you know what's going to happen?"

I felt sick in the pit of my stomach and a flutter of palpitations crossed my chest.

Constance hissed bushing out her coat.

"Maybe we should just talk it through this evening," I said. "And then plan the actual ghost zap for another occasion?"

Jeff's face fell. "I'd rather get it done tonight. I'll have to charge double if I need to come out again."

I guess there's no point in putting it off. I'll soon be entering the realms of my overdraft. I nodded and my mouth felt dry as I passed him a cup of tea and a plate with a warm brownie, a dollop of clotted cream and the necessary spoon. "How exactly will this work?" I asked.

Jeff shovelled in a mouthful of brownie and I waited whilst he chewed. He swallowed. "I'll start off with the equipment to gauge the best spot and then get the SLS going to check for ..." I guess he noticed my glazed expression. "You know what? Let's get the gear out of the van. It'll be easier for me to explain."

I put the front door on its latch and hurried to the curb, looking to see if there were any curtains twitching as I grabbed a wooden box out of the van. Constance sat on the front wall staring at me as if she disapproved. *Was this such a great idea?*

Once inside, amongst a pile of boxes, I turned to Constance who stared at Jeff as he pulled out his gadgets. I doubt she was going to like it once they started to make noises.

"I'll put the cat out the back," I said.

As I approached Constance, she growled and struggled in my arms as I picked her up.

"It's for your own good," I said as I shut her in the snug.

Back in the lounge, Jeff lifted up the grey handheld device, which I remembered from his first visit. "This is an EMF meter."

I raised my eyebrows. "The thing that flashes and makes a noise?"

"Hopefully, yes." He looked excited.

I bit my lip, feeling as if I was his evening entertainment. "This is quite real for me, Jeff. You might find this exciting," I pointed to his equipment. "But to me it's a nightmare I want to end."

"Sure, I get it." He shoved the EMF meter at me.

I took it in my hand. It had a dial on it. "How does it work?"

"It detects changes in the electromagnetic field." He shook his head as if to say *everyone knows that*. He pointed to the dial. "This will move up and the pitch will increase when spirits appear. I'll look for spikes in the EMF signal."

I frowned and gave a slow, "Okay."

Jeff rolled his eyes. "A spike in the electrical current will alert us to a spirit being."

"How do you know it's a spirit being and not some other kind of energy? Like the cat or something. What evidence is there that it does what you say?"

"Well there's no firm scientific evidence as such connecting the two. But trust me – it works." He put a tripod together and picked up what looked like a paparazzi camera. "Now this is an SLS Camera with an infrared light projector incorporating a monochrome CMOS sensor."

"Sounds interesting." *Just get on with it and stop showing off.*

Jeff scowled at me. I guess he may have detected the sarcasm in my voice.

"It 'sees' people. It detects paranormal entities that it recognises as a human shape based on the body parts and joints." He pointed to the screen. "There will be spirits shown on this display in stick person form."

I heard a pitiful kitty wail from the snug as I picked up my cup and took a sip of tea. "Looks like an expensive bit of kit."

Jeff nodded. "That's why I need to start the ghost hunts to pay for all of this." He grabbed his laptop. "Here's some footage from the Branden Arms." He brought up a video of a colourful bright green stick man flitting about the screen, like a really bad animation.

I sucked in my cheeks and tried not to laugh. "I see." I sighed, it seemed like a load of old clap trap. Although the smile disappeared from my face when I remembered I'd shelled out one hundred quid.

"I'll set up and then once something comes through, we can communicate with them and tell them to leave."

I watched him at work and shivered. Part of me wanted the shadow to appear so that we could move it on – but the other part never wanted to see the shadow again. I took a deep breath. *You can do this.*

. . .

COME TEN O'CLOCK, I'd had enough of Jeff in my house. We slouched on a sofa each having demolished more chocolate brownie. He stared at his EMF meter, which made noises here and there, but apparently not the right type of noises.

He glared at me. "You're going to have to help me out here."

"Me? Help?"

"Yes. Nothing is going to come through unless you make an effort."

I shook my head. "I don't know what to do. I never encourage them on purpose – you know that."

"Well, you're acting closed." He took in a deep breath and shook his head. "If you don't let him in, we can't ask him to move on. Can we?"

I felt a sickening ache inside and scratched my neck. "You're the one who said you'd come over here and sort it out. You didn't say I had to do anything." *I should ask for a discount; I didn't help the gardeners mow the lawn.*

"I thought it would have been obvious. You're the bridge – a door. Now let them know you're open for business."

I frowned. "The whole point is I don't want to use any paranormal power. That's why I'm not going through Lynn and her cult."

Jeff shook his head. "Just relax will you? And them lot over the back aren't a cult," he laughed.

This was a mistake. I sighed.

He softened his voice. "Hey, sorry. I only want to help you get this sorted."

"That's okay. I know what I need to do." I sat on the sofa and leaned back shutting my eyes. I took a deep breath in through my nose and exhaled for the count of ten. I kept doing this, focusing on a single vision in my mind of a simple white orchid. *Breathe in, two, three, four, five. Out, two, three, four, five, six, seven, eight, nine, ten.*

I began to drift off then opened my eyes with a jolt. The EMF machine bleeped in an erratic fashion. Jeff stood opposite me, staring at the digital display on his camera. His eyes were wide open and a grin spread across his face. "They're here," he said in a loud whisper which was just as spooky as the ghost – or ghosts – considering he spoke in the plural.

"They? It was just the one I was supposed to be connecting with," I said as painful static buzzed down my body. "Ouch."

"I've no idea who they are, but they're in the room." He rushed to the coffee table and opened a box, taking out what looked like a board game. All I could think of in my mind was *Jumanji*. My heart pulsed hard. *I don't like this. The house will get trashed if the movie is anything to go by.* Yes, the house was big but not large enough to accommodate a migration of elephants. *Forget the movies.* I scolded myself. I needed to remain level-headed at a time which was freaky enough without me adding to it.

Jeff opened the board, it had letters on it and he picked up a glass from his bag. "Right, come here."

I shook my head. "No way Jeff. Is that a Ouija board?"

He nodded.

"But they're dangerous."

"Not in the hands of an experienced practitioner. Sit down."

Experienced practitioner? The guy was not much more than a kid, I considered protesting but decided I'd come this far, I may as well go with it. I sat opposite him and watched my hand shake as I put a finger out. As soon as I touched the glass it shifted across the board. I scowled at Jeff and frowned.

He shook his head. "It's not me, it's them."

The glass sat at the letter Z. I knew what was coming next as it careered over to the O and then E. In quick succession the glass spelled out Z O E F I N D Z O E.

Jeff's eyes darted around the room. "You need to move on. Move towards the light. Becky has no business with you."

The glass sped to the N, followed by O. Then to N and O again. I pulled my hand, now full of pins and needles, away from the glass.

Jeff frowned "What?"

"I don't like it."

"It's not going to stop unless you deal with it now." He pointed to my hand. "Come on."

I put my finger back on the glass and it started to shake on the spot. "What's going on? Why won't it move?" The glass shot off the table and smashed against the wall. I shielded my eyes as glass shattered everywhere. *This is way too freaky.* The equipment screeched and lights flashed. I could hear Constance wailing from the snug and felt as if I wanted to rush to her.

Jeff stood up and looked through the view finder, "Oh, no. No way." He put his hand to his head.

"What? What's wrong?" I asked, thinking what a silly question that was – a lot was wrong. Static coursed through my body from all angles as if I'd been plugged into the mains.

"There's too much here." Jeff stepped back glancing through his camera.

"What do you mean?" I shouted as ringing pierced my ears. I felt the room spinning and saw shadows swirling around as if I was in the kitchen sink and the plug had been pulled. *Great, I'm gonna get flushed away.*

Jeff ran around the room like a headless chicken. "I'll get help," he shouted as he rushed out.

Oh, brilliant. I felt rooted to the spot. "Don't just leave me," I called out. But he'd gone. "Stop, stop, stop," I shouted. The room fell silent, I looked around. The equipment lights had dimmed and there was only a constant beep from the EMF meter.

Something moved in the left of my eye. I turned and saw a girl, sitting in the corner of the room, hugging her knees, her head facing downwards. She wasn't a shadow, she shone like a polished sculpture.

My breath was visible in the oddly icy air. I could hear Constance's meow in the distance. In my head, one name was repeated. *Zoe*. Her hair was cut into a bob style, glistening like silver. Her skin pale. Her head slowly moved upwards until she faced me, her eyes like marbles, were shiny as if she'd been crying for an eternity. My fear dissipated in that moment overtaken by an urge to help her. I knew, if I helped Zoe, I would be free and so would she.

"Where are you?" I asked.

Her voice was faint and I strained to hear it. "I would ..."

The door swung open and, in a flash, the vision disappeared and the room fell silent, No trace of anything ghostly.

"I thought my mobile was in the van, but I can't find it. Can I borrow yours? I'll phone Lynn."

I shook my head and stood up. "No. Jeff. Leave it. They've gone."

Jeff looked around; everything was silent apart from Constance's meow coming from the snug. "I'll let you have a refund. Sorry Becky," he stuttered as he packed away his things his head low "We could try again?"

I shook my head. "No thanks." *I should have known better than to hire a virgin paranormal investigator.*

As I helped him return the equipment to his van, I realised the only way I was going to stop this, was to find Zoe myself, in the real world. To find her body, her resting place.

CHAPTER 11

*A*t seven the next morning I leaned on my front wall and yawned as I watched seagulls attack a waste bin on the prom. The sea was so calm it looked like a pond and there was no breeze. The temperature was fresh and the sky was a clear blue. The odd car drove by every now and again and a solitary dog walker strolled along the sands. Constance rubbed her head on my hand for a stroke. She'd been at my side constantly since I'd let her out of the snug the previous evening. I found it comforting. I had to admit, the night before had been off-the-scale weird. But it was a realisation – *yes, I can connect to the other side.* Whilst I was ready to admit I had this gift I was certainly not interested in using it. And I felt troubled by the fact that Grandma had never mentioned her spiritual gift to me, before she died. But I knew she had loved me with all her heart and guessed she had just wanted to protect me. Maybe she had not wanted me to develop this gift, and I certainly didn't want that either, which is why I decided to help find Zoe by extracting information out of the living – that would eliminate the need to speak to the dead.

I checked the road to see if I could spot H. Whilst initially, I'd had no intention of going for a run with him, I realised he would be a good source of information if I was ever to find Zoe and rid myself of the hauntings.

I wore a pair of leggings and a t-shirt, not owning any running clothes. *Why on earth did I agree to a run?* I could have said a walk along the beach maybe? Hopefully H would realise the run would be at jogging-pace. The only time I'd broken into a sprint over the past year was to catch a bus.

I glanced down at my sparkly fashion trainers. Money was tight and it was unlikely this run would become a regular thing, certainly not worth the purchase of a regular pair of running shoes. I looked to my right as a brown baby gull cried out from the sea wall. In the distance there was a man striding towards me. *Definitely H.*

"Hi there," he said a couple of minutes later as he reached my house, dressed in black. *What is he wearing?* I thought, *or not wearing. This guy must seriously work out.* He had those flimsy type of running shorts, the ones that show when someone has muscly – very muscly in this instance – thighs. He'd teamed that with a black vest. I didn't know where to look.

He grinned at me as he jogged on the spot. "Right, where do you usually go?"

"Er, up the High Street." Which was true, but usually with my tote bag over my arm when the shops were open.

"Great, an uphill run. I'll follow you."

I began jogging and Constance jumped along the wall beside me. It didn't seem so bad. I could feel him at my side but kept my eyes straight ahead. Reaching the corner of the High Street I had set a sensible pace, considering the speed needed to sustain a run for probably half an hour. My thighs started to burn after we'd passed a couple of shops, it was after all an uphill climb. I didn't want to slow down and make myself look weak. My chest felt a little tight. I wondered how Mr Fit was doing. I could hear him puffing so I looked to my left.

I realised his puff was more of a laugh. His eyes danced and were creased at the sides. With the sun shining in them, the pupils were much smaller and I could see they were a soft shade of brown. It was then I realised that whilst I was running, he was only walking in big strides.

The air in my lungs seemed to disappear all at once and I had a burning sensation in my gut. I stopped. "I don't think this is going to work is it? Your legs are much longer than mine."

He laughed. "Are you okay?"

"It must be hay fever or something." I rubbed my chest and faked a little sneeze.

"Right." He grinned. "Maybe we'll just take a walk? Rather than work up a sweat?"

I wondered how many women H had worked up a sweat with, then pushed that out of my mind. *I won't be going there.*

He even walked quickly compared to me. I felt as if I were trotting beside him like a pet chihuahua. I paused and held my side as a stitch formed and glanced behind me. Constance had stopped following us. She stared at me then turned back, her fluffy tail in the air as she sashayed away. Constance was clearly not the only one who didn't fancy such unnecessary and excessive exercise.

"I'll take you up the top and show you where all the rich live," H said.

I knew where he meant. Set behind the residential streets, which ran parallel to the beach, was a hill upon which Branden Bay's Castle sat, which had been built five hundred years ago. Next to this a wood had been planted by the Victorians to soften the landscape. At over one hundred years old, the wood was now dense with all sorts of different bushes and trees. I'd been up there a few times with Grandma, collecting blackberries for her most delicious blackberry and apple crumble. She also made a yummy vanilla custard. My stomach rumbled as I visualised the food and I wished that H had invited me for a full English breakfast rather than this uphill trudge.

I looked ahead as we approached Upper Ashcombe Road, which ran along the edge of the wood, where the grandest houses in town were situated. Most of them were huge detached Victorian villas commanding excellent views over the town and sea towards Wales.

As we walked along the poshest road in town, H stopped every now and again, pointing out where the local MP lived, the parish vicarage and the home of the town's famous rock star. He also showed me a house that had suffered a fire and been rebuilt.

I was relieved when we reached a bench, which had a full view of the bay. H sat down and I perched next to him. My poor legs ached and my feet burned, which served me right for wearing fashion trainers. I had to do some serious shopping. *I need a job and quick.*

"I sit here often," he said. "It's a great view of town." He paused. "Zoe used to live up here."

I looked at him sharply. Having heard her name a shot of static shot up my spine.

"She was only sixteen when she went missing. We were all just kids really."

It was worth the effort, I thought. *Here goes.* "It must have been a frightening time for you all. I guess that sort of thing stays with you forever." A part of me felt guilty, pushing him for information when it clearly brought back bad memories.

"It's the not knowing that eats me up. Not knowing

what happened to her." H shook his head. "And it's not just me. It's the same for Annie and Izzy. It's always there, a scar we cover up, but I still feel it when we're together – although we never talk about it. Not usually."

The guy was really opening up. It seemed a real contrast to the big and beefy exterior.

"So where do you think she is?" I asked.

H sat back and crossed his arms. "I don't know. But I'm sure she wouldn't have run away. That's what the Police decided at the time. Her father had disappeared a week before, so they presumed she'd joined him. He'd broken up with her step-mother, following an argument over money. She said he'd skipped town with her life savings, leaving Zoe with her."

"So Zoe stayed with her step-mum?"

"Yes, then soon after she disappeared too."

"Maybe she went off looking for her dad?"

"I can't imagine she'd leave without saying something to at least one of us. If you ask me, it had something to do with her step-mum. She hated her. She called her the step-witch and I never trusted that woman. There was always something evil about her. And I don't believe Thomas would have stolen money from anyone. It doesn't add up. The step-mother had something to do with it."

"So why did the police think she ran away?"

H ran a hand through his hair. "When they searched the house, her rucksack, some clothes and her passport were missing. And as her step-mother was convinced Zoe had sloped off to meet Thomas, there was no further reason for the police to continue their enquiries."

"But you wanted to know where Zoe was?"

"Annie, Izzy and me we were just kids back then. No-one took us seriously."

"But wasn't it the talk of the town?"

"Yes, the Gazette picked up on it but it never made the nationals. Thousands of people go missing every year, running away to large towns in the hope of making a new life for themselves." He gestured across the horizon. "The fact that most people around here thought that there was something dodgy afoot, especially as far as her step-mother was concerned, wasn't enough to warrant any further investigation."

I felt sick and a twinge of static nipped at my neck.

H sighed. "If she was alive, she would have contacted me. Or at least one of us. We think she ..." H ran a hand through his hair. "To me, the mystery isn't whether or not she ran away. I feel in here," he thumped his chest. "She's dead."

I had to agree. I wouldn't have seen her ghost the previous evening if she was still alive. But I kept that fact to myself. I rubbed my arms. The bench was in the shade and the sea breeze blew in. The tide must have turned.

H stood up. "Without a body the case will never be

reopened. If they found her body, the mystery will be solved."

The words, *find Zoe,* echoed in my head. "What happened to her step-mother?"

H nodded up the road. "She still lives here but she's leaving soon. The house is on the market."

I stood up, my legs ached. "What house?"

H turned to his right. "The one with the stone balcony."

It was a huge detached villa backing onto the woods. I began to walk in that direction.

H called me back. "Let's not go that way. I need to head back now."

"Sure." I followed him in the direction of the bay.

As I caught up with him he smiled at me. "Sorry to be so depressing. I feel I can talk about it to you. Probably because you're from out of town and don't know the history."

I smiled. "No worries, if it feels good to talk about it."

He smiled at me and I felt a tingle in my body – I looked around hoping there were no spirits nearby. I slapped a smile on my face but as we started our descent to the bay, I decided the next thing I would do in my quest to find Zoe was to check out her old house.

· · ·

BACK HOME, I paced the snug. Constance meowed at me. I picked her up and petted her as she fluffed out her fur and meowed even louder.

"What?" I asked.

She wriggled free to the ground, sashayed through the open French windows and headed up the garden. I followed her fluffy body until she reached the closed door in the back wall.

"Wait, What? You want me to open the door for you?" I crossed my arms. "You're quite capable of jumping over the top." *This cat's got some cheek, treating me like its servant.*

She turned and meowed loudly and I put my hands to my ears.

"For goodness sake," I said as I grabbed the large metal handle and twisted it. As I opened the door, I jumped.

Lynn stood before me. "Well hello, lovey. What a nice surprise."

"Hi, Lynn," I said. *Thanks, Constance.*

"I was going to pop around and see you. Annie asked me if I could lend you some tables for your café?"

"It's a charity tea for the neighbours. I'm not opening a café."

"We'll see about that, lovey." She winked at me. "Anyway, of course you can borrow the tables and I've a list of neighbours you can invite. Do you want to pop in for a cuppa?"

"Thanks, but I'm busy designing my invites."

"That's a shame."

Lynn pulled a typed list out of her pocket and passed it to me. "How are you sleeping, deary?"

"Fine. I seem to have got over my er ... problems."

Lynn raised her eyebrows. "Well, if there are any issues, remember don't hesitate to ask. There's all sorts I can do."

I don't doubt that, I thought. But I wanted to deal with this matter in the living world, I'd had enough ghostly experiences to last a lifetime and I was a little wary that she wanted to use me to contact Zoe. I thanked Lynn and headed back to my house.

As I reached the snug, my phone rang. I picked it up from the table. *Wendy calling.* I smiled as I answered it, I'd texted asking her to call me when she was free for a chat.

"Hi Wendy. I wondered how many of your society will be coming for the afternoon tea?"

"I've drummed up a lot of business for you. There'll be twenty-two of us."

"Twenty-two? Wow, that'll pretty much fill the place up."

"Indeed. I wondered whether you wanted to do a separate sitting for us?"

"That's an excellent idea. I'll update the leaflet to ask people to book ahead."

"Perfect, the ladies are really keen. They already

want to book you as a judge for our next baking competition."

"Oh dear, pressure," I laughed.

"It's going to be a resounding success, I'm sure of it."

"Do you want to pop over tomorrow morning and help drop some leaflets?" I wanted to see Wendy again and it would be nice to have company on the leaflet drop.

"I'd love to dear but I have appointments for most of tomorrow. I could do the following day?"

"Okay, I'll let you know how I get on tomorrow and maybe we'll meet up another time."

"Definitely," she said.

I replaced the phone on the table and felt a little deflated as I reached for my laptop. I wanted to confide in her about the whole Zoe thing. I needed to find someone I could be honest with – and whilst I could do that with Jeff, he had a little bit too much of an interest in the paranormal for my liking. I opened up the laptop and got to work.

Three hours later, I was happy with my design for the leaflets. I'd prepared them invitation style, placing an image of a cake stand full of treats, followed with:

Becky James invites you
for afternoon tea and cake
on the 5th of July
at 32 Beach Road.

£12.50 per person
All profits donated to Branden Bay Hospice Care
Booking is essential.

Underneath I gave my telephone number. It looked pretty smart and I pointed to the screen and then grabbed Constance to stop her walking over my keyboard. "What do you think of this, Connie cat?" She purred and nuzzled my hand so I stroked her head. I guessed she approved.

Constance watched the printer with interest as it spat out each sheet of paper. I printed two invitations per sheet and cut them neatly with a pair of scissors. I was all set – the following day I would spend delivering leaflets and I now had the perfect excuse to walk right up to the front door of Zoe's old house.

CHAPTER 12

It had been a productive morning and having posted leaflets through the imme-diate neighbouring houses, I turned into the High Street, then cut down Castle Road where Lynn's hut and Annie's apartment were. Lynn had given me the house numbers of those people she thought would be interested. Constance meowed from my bag, having jumped in there again. I scratched her head; she was light and easy to carry, even if her fur took up a lot of bag space. I decided to pop into Branden Bay Pet Store on the way back to look for a more suitable bag. I remembered seeing a woman a few days before with a miniature poodle in a pet bag with a window, which was much more appropriate for a cat than a Givenchy.

Castle Road snaked up the hill. It wasn't the most direct route but there were a few addresses on the road which Lynn had given me. Finally, in Upper Ashcombe

Road I stopped for breath. I was certainly getting my quota of exercise that day. The traffic was a lot lighter there, so I pulled Constance out of my bag. "I'm not going to be able to carry you up the hill. You can walk this stretch."

She trotted at my side for a while until I reached the bench I'd sat on with H, Zoe's house was only a few doors up. I sat down, summoning up the courage to commence snooping. Constance jumped back into the bag. *Cheeky.* I pulled out a leaflet, I needed to make it look legit. *Here goes.* I studied each house as I passed. Most were detached with two or three floors. Some with gargoyles and griffins carved into stone. Having passed a grand villa which had been converted into three swanky flats, I approached Zoe's house. Up close, I could see it was tired and in need of attention. A winding drive meandered through tatty gardens. I stopped at the bottom of the drive looking up. I saw there was a 'for sale' sign. *This is definitely the house.* I jumped as I heard a car door slam and a voice behind me.

"Mrs Abercrombie? You're early."

I turned around and saw a man in a very snappy suit smiling at me. He looked mid-thirties and held a folder with *Emerson's Estate Agents* on it.

"Stephen Dodds." He nodded at me.

"Oh. Hi."

"Was your flight from Edinburgh smooth?"

I nodded. *Scotland?*

"So," he looked at his notes. "You're moving to the area and looking for a place for your growing family?" He glanced at my stomach.

I turned to gaze up at the house. I had a choice, I could tell him I was stopping by to deliver a leaflet about my charity event. Or I could pretend to be the prospective buyer.

"Aye," I replied, going for the latter option. I took a deep breath. *I can do this.* I racked my brain for a Scottish woman to impersonate. Mrs Doubtfire, was the first that came to mind. Okay, the character was a middle-aged man but it was only the accent I needed to summon up, not the look. My heart thudded. *"The bairns will love the milder climate."*

"Let's get started then," Stephen smiled.

I looked down at Constance in my bag. Her eyes were wide open, staring up at me. I doubt she would be jumping out again having climbed up the hill. I squeezed the bag closer to me, to hide the contents and pushed down a clump of ginger fluff which had poked out. I prayed that Zoe's step-mother didn't have a dog. As I followed Stephen up the drive, my legs trembled. I looked at the top of Constance's head, wondering if curiosity did indeed kill the cat.

Stephen walked ahead of me, saying over his shoulder. "It's in a beautiful position with outstanding views of the bay and it backs onto the woods. There's a sturdy gate at the back, it's completely secure." He looked around. "You're not overlooked by anyone."

I followed him. My legs ached as we climbed the drive back and forth around the bends.

"There are steps which provide a more direct route to the house but they need rebuilding. I don't think you would want to tackle them in your er ... condition."

I smiled sweetly wondering what ailment Mrs Abercrombie had.

Once we reached the house I looked up at the double-fronted building. It appeared even bigger up close. It had a patio area looking out over the bay.

Stephen checked his clip board. "In your email you said that you were looking for this to be your family home. You have two and another on the way?"

Oh dear. I pulled my dark sunglasses on and clutched the now wriggling bag in front of my belly.

"I must say. You don't look old enough to have children at secondary school."

Teenagers? Wow. "I'm flattered. They're twins," I said then did the mathematics and realised I could never pass as mother to teenagers. "And I'm a step-parent."

"I see. They must be a handful."

I remembered how Grandma had told me, don't lie, because one small lie leads to many more. "Aye, they are. And I have a nanny."

"The vendor is out, so it will be only me showing you around."

Perfect. I breathed out and relaxed. "Okay, although I don't have that much time."

I heard a meow from the bag and I looked around. *Maybe I should scarper now.* Leave before I slipped up. But I wanted to see inside, to get a feel for the place. *Maybe the body was hidden here?* I glanced down at my feet and shuddered. "How many years has this patio been down?"

Stephen frowned.

Okay, maybe not the best question.

"I'm not sure. I'll ask Mrs. Palmer." He opened the front door and it creaked. "There are two entrances. Due to the size of the property, the vendor has only been living in part of the house. This will certainly be a project for the new owner but it will be a handsome home once renovated. As you can see, it needs a lot more than a touch of TLC." He looked me up and down. "Do you have any experience of renovations?"

"My husband has a building company." *Another lie.*

"Really?" Stephen frowned. "As well as being a transatlantic pilot?"

Oh dear. "The building company is the family business, he's on the board of directors." The lies were piling up. "Is there any scope for movement on the price?" I'd spent a fair few hours watching re-runs of house-buying TV shows during the long nights.

Stephen nodded. "I think she might drop a little."

I heard another meow. "Seems as if the vendor has a cat somewhere," I said glaring down at Constance as Stephen looked away.

"Strange, I've not noticed any pets before." Stephen frowned.

We walked into the hallway, where floral paper was peeling off the walls. The staircase was wide and I could picture in my mind young women with fancy Victorian dresses sweeping down with their hair in ringlets. Even in a state of disrepair the grandness spoke out.

We approached the first room, Stephen walked ahead of me. Wood panelling ran up the sides of the bay window, which was water stained and full of mildew. There was no furniture.

Stephen motioned his arms around. "This was the original dining room."

I walked towards the window. "Amazing views." I could see the full bay. To the far right was Millars Hotel and Spa, standing proud with its windows twinkling in the sun. Further on, the road gradually rose up the hill. I turned to the left to view the fun fair at the opposite end of the bay, with its helter-skelter and Ferris wheel with the pier jutting out. Beyond that, the Mendip Hills rose and I saw the small oblongs of caravans and lodges in the distance on the Branden Bay Holiday Park. The tide was fully in, with white crests on the waves. I remembered why I'd loved coming here so much in the summer holidays.

"Stunning view, isn't it?" Stephen said bringing me out of my daydream. "Seen enough?"

I nodded. "Yeah," I said in my London accent then

followed it up with an over-pronounced, "Aye."
Remember – stay in character.

"The next room is the main living space."

I followed Stephen into the lounge which was huge
and furnished, as if it had been left to wither. "Looks
like something off an old film."

"Yes. I think she couldn't face clearing it – after
what happened."

I stopped and looked at him. "What happened?"
Time to act ignorant.

Stephen shifted his feet, eyeing me as if wondering
whether to mention it or not. "Her family disappeared." He visibly shuddered.

"Sounds mysterious."

"Erm. Yeah." Stephen's Adam's apple bobbed up
and down. Local gossip clearly had something more
sinister than the official verdict that Zoe had ran away
with her father.

"Intriguing." I raised my eyebrows. "I see there are
a lot of original features, the cornicing, the picture
rails. The fireplace."

Stephen smiled. "Yes, it's a unique property, so many
people ripped out the Victorian touches in the fifties,
modernising everything. It's nice to see them intact."

We carried on through the rest of the ground floor.
Same story, rooms with no life, left to ruin.

"So why is the vendor selling now?" I asked.

"She's moving to Spain."

"Why has she remained here this long? It must have taken years for it to deteriorate to this extent?"

Stephen gave a short cough. "I'll leave the vendor to explain through her solicitor should you wish to proceed and need further details."

"I see." I had the impression that Stephen knew exactly the reason and was choosing to remain tight-lipped.

We walked towards the stairs and Stephen passed me, leading the way. I felt a scrabbling in my bag. Constance appeared restless, I peered in and she jumped out. I took a sharp intake of breath and watched as she overtook Stephen and climbed the stairs.

"Oi," I called out in my natural accent, forgetting the softly spoken Doubtfire-esque tones.

Stephen stopped his ascent. "Oh, it appears Mrs Palmer does indeed have a pet. Odd, I've never seen it before."

"Och, what a wee bonnie cat," I said reinforcing the Scottish tones as I scowled at Constance who turned and then carried on with her signature sashay up to the first floor. Hopefully I would be able to sneak her back into my bag when we got up there. We followed Constance up the wide sweeping staircase towards the bedrooms. All doors were open apart from one. Constance wandered over to the closed door and scratched at it.

Stephen led me to the bathroom. "This bathroom is one of the grandest in the house."

I walked in. "Beautiful tub," I said as I pointed to the roll top bath with tarnished gold taps. Inside was a fire place and a huge sink with an ornate gold framed mirror above. I looked back into the hall as I heard a long wail from Constance. I crossed the landing towards the shut door which she continued to scrape at. I reached for the knob and as my hand came into contact with it, I felt static shoot up my arm. It was locked. "What's in this room?" I asked.

"The vendor discourages me from showing it. It's full of personal effects."

I raised my eyebrows. "I'd like to see the full house. I'm a serious buyer and have had a long journey." *Massive lie.*

Stephen scratched his nose and looked down the stairs. "Well, as she's not here to ask." He fumbled with the keys and unlocked the door. As it creaked open, I felt a breeze touch my face. I shivered as I looked inside. Constance hissed. I heard the sound of foot-steps drift up from the ground floor. Stephen turned; his eyes widened as he moved forward to pull the door closed. But not before I saw it – the picture on the dresser. It loomed up to me as if I'd looked at it through binoculars. It was of a girl with a blonde bob and a large man with his arm around her shoulders, wearing a Panama hat. Zoe and her dad. *Thomas is the shadow.* I knew at that moment that this meant he was definitely dead too.

"Stephen?" A woman's voice called. It sounded familiar.

Stephen quickly locked the door and I crouched down opening the bag for Constance to jump into while he was distracted.

"I'm here, Mrs Palmer. I'm showing Mrs Abercrombie the bedrooms."

"I don't think so, Stephen, as Mrs. Abercrombie is here – standing beside me."

Uh oh. I gulped and my heart raced. *I've really gone and done it now.*

CHAPTER 13

S tephen glared at me as we stood outside the
bedroom door.

"Who are you?" He hissed.

An equally demanding hiss came from my bag as I
stuffed Constance into it. "I just wanted to look
around," I said, the Scottishness now completely lost
from my voice.

Stephen shook his head and took his handkerchief
from his pocket to mop his brow. "I said – who are
you?" His face was so beetroot that mine coloured up
in sympathy, he appeared petrified of this woman. This
did not make me feel any better. But we couldn't just
stand there, I had to do something.

"Stephen?" Mrs. Palmer's voice was shrill and
abrupt.

I stood up straight and turned to him. "It's my fault,

leave it to me." I needed to tap into my acting skills, yet again. *I knew that degree would come in handy someday.* I descended the stairs with the feeling that I'd have to blag and run. As I approached the sweeping bend, I pictured a miserable woman with bushy dark hair dressed in an A-line skirt and jumper with a large hammer and a knife. But as I turned the bend of the stairs, I was surprised by what I saw at the bottom.

There was a smart glamorous lady, with smooth dark locks, not dissimilar to Wendy. A lot like Wendy. *Oh! It is Wendy.* I put my hand to my mouth.

Wendy took a step back and I saw a flicker of something in her eyes. Was she angry? Surprised? Scared? But her face instantly softened.

"Becky, dear. What on earth are you doing here?"

"I'm so sorry." My palms were sweating. "I was delivering leaflets for the afternoon tea and I saw this house, which looked so charming and beautiful. And then when Stephen asked if I was here to look around, without thinking I just said yes." I put my hand to my chest. "I had no idea it was your property." *Now that's the truth.* "I feel awful. It was so rude of me."

The penny suddenly dropped. Wendy, lovely Wendy, the person who reminded me of my mum and gave me a warm fuzzy feeling inside, was Zoe's stepwitch? This was the woman H had painted as evil?

"I see," she said.

"You get nothing like this in London, with the

views." I looked to the porch where a tall and extremely pregnant lady stood, wearing a green maternity dress suit.

Mrs Abercrombie was not smiling.

"Sorry," I said. "I didn't realise I was taking someone else's appointment. I assumed it was open house. I feel dreadfully cheeky."

Wendy looked over my shoulder to Stephen who I could hear descending the stairs behind me. "Stephen. Maybe you should have explained that it was not open house."

I looked around to him and mouthed, *sorry*.

"Double appointments are fine but please don't leave prospective buyers out in the street if you're running late. It's rude and so unprofessional." Wendy pursed her crimson painted lips.

I squeezed my bag as I felt Constance move inside. "I take full responsibility, it's not his fault." I turned to Mrs. Abercrombie. "Please accept my sincere apology." I reached into my bag. If this woman could afford a huge house and hubby was a pilot, I was sure she could splash out at the charity do. I handed her an invitation. "If you want to suss out the local area, why not come along to my afternoon tea?"

Mrs. Abercrombie took a sharp intake of breath. "I'm only in town today looking at property." I noted that there was not a trace of Scottishness in her overly posh voice – she definitely wasn't Mrs Doubtfire.

"Stephen, if you could show Mrs. Abercrombie around and I'll deal with Becky."

Deal with? I swallowed hard. That didn't sound good.

Stephen approached Mrs Abercrombie. "Come this way, we'll start with the dining room and I do apologise," he said, glaring at me as he led the prospective buyer away.

Wendy shook her head and laughed. "You're a little minx, aren't you?"

"I guess I've been well and truly busted."

Wendy slipped her arm in mine. "Why don't you come and have coffee with me and tell me how you're getting along with your plans for the afternoon tea?"

Phew, I seemed to have been forgiven. "I don't want to intrude."

"Nonsense. I rarely have visitors. And we're friends. You must join the Branden Bay Ladies' Society, we can pop along to the hall when Stephen's finished the viewing and pick you up a registration form."

H must be mistaken; I could tell, Wendy was a genuinely lovely lady.

"Follow me." She directed me outside.

As I stepped out I tipped Constance out of my bag, she hissed annoyed at being turfed out of her cosy space.

Wendy jumped. "Where did she come from?"

"Sorry, she follows me everywhere." I pointed at Constance. "You'll have to wait for me here, Connie."

Constance sat down and watched as I followed Wendy inside.

"You seem to have her well trained," Wendy said as she led me to a side door. "Now, I'm not sure how much Stephen told you, but I only live in the annex. The house was far too big for just me."

I followed her in and up a short flight of stairs to an apartment. I wondered whether I should confess that I knew her history, but decided to act clueless. It would be easier to play dumb. The annex was a total contrast to the big gloomy house and was bright and homely. She led me to the first room – a kitchen diner with modern units which was decked out with flashy appliances.

"Sit down."

I did as I was told.

"Do you know the history of this house?"

I gulped. "History?"

"Have you been told any stories about me?"

I frowned, hoping my expression did not give me away. Heat gradually crept up my neck. "I'm not really up on the local gossip. Are you a celebrity?"

Wendy shook her head, her eyes lowered. "I was just checking; I have to be so careful you see. I've been the subject of a smear campaign."

I felt rather guilty, playing it dumb when Wendy had clearly been through the mill. "Really? Why's that?" I found 'acting' tricky when I could not pretend to be someone else. I was a cool, calm and collected Mrs. Abercrombie, but lying as Becky was difficult.

"My husband and step-daughter left me and even though the police confirmed this to be the case, the locals still had me down as some sort of evil killer," she said smoothing down her dark glossy locks. "There was talk that I'd disposed of their bodies in an acid bath, amongst other theories."

I gulped, remembering the large roll top bath I'd seen. *I wonder how much acid you'd need? No wonder the taps were tarnished.* "That's so cruel," I said, then quickly added, "the lies and gossip I mean, not melting their bodies, because of course you didn't do that." I realised I had started to ramble and hoped that Wendy didn't think I was a meddling amateur sleuth.

Is that what I am? If I was, I wasn't a very good one. Wendy blinked as if to see off tears. I felt guilty. *This is her real life,* I thought, telling myself off. *What on earth am I doing?*

"It indeed was cruel, especially as I had to come to terms with the loss of my family. Whilst I may have been fed up with Thomas before he left, I still loved him. And dear Zoe. I brought her up as my own. She's the only child I've ever had. Even though I didn't give birth to her, I still felt she was mine. It was terribly heart-breaking and on top of that – being left with little money and the responsibility for the upkeep of the house." She wiped her eyes with a hankie. "I couldn't move because I was unable to sell the property as Thomas owned half." She looked at me straight in the eye. "Why on earth would I kill him? It makes no sense whatsoever."

"It doesn't," I said. She certainly had a point there. It would have been much simpler to just divorce the guy.

"I've finally got the go-ahead from my solicitor to sell up and keep the proceeds. It's been an uphill struggle." She shook her head. "Maybe I was too quick to accept the verdict that Thomas and Zoe ran away. What if they did die? I guess now we'll never know."

Poor Wendy. She was the first person in Branden Bay that I'd got to know and now I felt it was not just Zoe and Thomas I wanted to help solve this. If the bodies were found, it could give a clue as to who the real killer was. "Stephen said you were moving away?"

"Yes, the long term plan is to move to the Spanish Costa del Sol. If the place sells, that is."

"It's bound to sell. It's a beautiful house."

"The place is disintegrating. It'll be nice if someone brings it back to its former glory."

"You never mentioned this to me at our tea the other day."

"Becky, I've got used to people not trusting me. That's why it's so nice to meet someone new, who isn't prejudiced against me."

"So, why do people think you killed them? It's a bit far-fetched."

Wendy sighed. "I had a massive row with Thomas.

I loved him so much but he had ploughed my savings and money inherited from my family into a new business he was trying out and it never took off. In a matter of months, most of my savings were gone. Before then I had enough wealth for us to live on without any worry. I guess it was greed which made Thomas take chances with a high-risk investment. Trying to prove himself, I suppose. I had my suspicions that he'd kept some of the money to abscond with. He left the house in a rage after our row and then the next morning when I woke, I noticed that he'd taken his passport with him. Initially I wondered if it was just for ID purposes but after a week he never showed and then Zoe disappeared too. Again, she'd taken her passport. At the time, I assumed he'd come back for her and I never heard from them again. I always fantasised that once Zoe became an adult and independent from her father, she'd come back to me. But she didn't. In recent years I worry that maybe she hadn't gone off with Thomas after all. Maybe something dreadful happened to her."

I could see her eyes filling with tears. Thomas and Zoe were obviously dead, I knew that. But there was no point in me confirming Wendy's fears.

"Who would have wanted to do any harm to her?"

Wendy shook her head. "I don't know. Maybe Thomas had run away from someone who was after him and it was punishment? But if it wasn't that ... I would guess it was something to do with Henry."

"Henry?"

"Her boyfriend at the time."

So that's what H stands for.

"They had him in for questioning."

Did they? "I thought you said the police were of the opinion she'd run away?"

"Not when I first reported her missing."

H had omitted that piece of information when we'd chatted. My mouth felt dry.

"I overheard Zoe arranging to meet him and when they checked the phone records he was the last person she'd spoken to. Then she disappeared."

I sat back and bit my lip. *H? A killer?*

"At the time, he was the prime suspect, not me. The police never saw me as a suspect. I was a victim but then that boy turned everyone against me."

"Really?" I was seeing H in a new light.

"It's all a smokescreen with him. I don't doubt that he's the one responsible for my bad reputation."

"Why do you say that?"

Wendy dabbed her eyes. "He's been a thorn in my side for years. I had to report him for harassment. And then he joined the police force." She threw her hands up. "What hope did I have?"

This was not looking good.

I put my head on one side. "But you're President of the Branden Bay Ladies' Society. They must respect you?"

"Yes, I've been accepted back into the social circles these days. But people take care to keep their distance.

No-one ever invites me to their home for tea, not like you, dear. That's why it was so lovely to meet you, Becky." Wendy poured filter coffee into the awaiting mugs. "Other people don't fully connect with me and what hurts most is that I can see they're frightened – as if I'm some sort of monster." She handed me a cup.

I felt heat rising up my face. I took it and thanked her.

"You're not frightened of me, Becky dear. Are you?"

"Of course not," I said and then took a gulp of the hot drink, burning my tongue.

"So, enough about me. Have you made any friends?"

I nearly spluttered my coffee. *Oh dear,* I didn't want to tell her I'd made friends with Zoe's mates. Especially not H, for goodness sake. "I've only been here for a couple of weeks."

"Well, you have a friend in me," she smiled. "And you're the loveliest person I've met in a long time. A real credit to your grandmother, my dear."

There was a knock at the door.

"Come in." Wendy slapped a smile on her face and stood up, smoothing her clothes down.

The door opened and Stephen appeared. "Is it okay if I show Mrs Abercrombie this part of the property?"

He scowled at me. I gave him a finger wiggling wave and a wide grin.

"Of course," said Wendy.

Mrs Abercrombie walked through and they made

general conversation about Branden Bay and the facilities it had on offer as I sipped my coffee. I looked out of the window and saw Constance waiting for me. I'd gathered enough information for now. It was time to leave and digest what I'd heard, my brain buzzed with contradicting information.

Once Stephen and the prospective buyer had left the room, I stood up. "I'd better be going actually. Thanks, Wendy, for the coffee."

"Oh, so soon?" She looked genuinely disappointed. "I wanted us to pop to the Ladies' Society hall."

"I have baking to do," I said, which was the truth, I needed to practice my bakes and plan for the afternoon tea which was turning into a bit of an extravaganza. I also needed to decide how to decorate and set the room.

Once I had bade her farewell, I stepped outside and let out a long breath as I walked up to Constance who was sitting at the top of the drive. She gave a long meow.

"It's not my fault you had to stay out here."

Constance sat rooted to the spot. I sighed, then lowered my bag and she jumped in.

As I walked down the hill towards home, I felt sick. It was hard to imagine petite, warm and friendly Wendy as a killer. Whilst the police eventually concluded that Zoe had ran away, what if H had something to do with it? I bit my lip. He certainly looked a lot more physically equipped to carry out a murder than a dainty woman like Wendy.

I shook my head; I was sure H wasn't in the frame but I needed another opinion. *Maybe Izzy?* I decided she would be the best person, seeing as she was brutally honest about my cake and considering the historic tension between Izzy and H, *she might be prepared to spill some beans.*

CHAPTER 14

I dusted icing sugar over what had to be my best Victoria sponge yet. I had finally mastered it, creating one that rose beautifully with an even bake. My previous attempts either had a cracked dome on top, or a pit in the middle. I'd since discovered it was all down to pan size, and the new tins I'd had delivered as part of my shopping channel spree had been my saviour.

I gave myself a pat on the back. *I'm getting pretty good at this.* I'd also made sure I didn't add too much baking powder after Izzy's scathing attack on my fudge cake. Whilst I had been none too chuffed at the time, she'd been right, I had put too much in. My mobile phone rang again and I reached for my planner – I'd already had a lot of interest for the charity tea and the slots were filling up.

After I'd taken the booking, the doorbell chimed. Constance trotted to the door, behaving as if she owned the place. I'd lured Izzy over by asking her opinion on a selection of the cakes I had planned to serve at the charity tea. It was sensible to get honest feedback anyway, as well as an opportunity to grill her about H and Wendy, my two main suspects.

Izzy glided through my house, raising her eyebrows. "Impressive," she said as she followed me into the snug. "You have such a divine home." Looking down at Constance she smiled. "Hello, little sweetie." She blew her a kiss.

We sat at the table in the snug with the French windows wide open. Constance settled down in the sun and cleaned herself.

Izzy touched my shoulder. "I wanted to apologise for the other night, darling. Insulting your fudge cake."

"No worries. You were right about the baking powder though. I've been working on my recipes and that was a bit of an experiment. It was far from perfect."

"So what would you like my opinion on today?" she said smiling.

"I'll get the cakes. I have three teas for you to taste as well."

Izzy reached into her bag. "I'll get my notebook out then."

"I hope I'm not taking up too much of your time."

"Of course not." She batted her eyelashes, they were long, mascaraed but clearly natural. Izzy would make Helen of Troy feel like a frump.

After three trips, to and from the kitchen, I had all of the cake slices laid out and three cups of tea.

I watched Izzy raise each cake in turn to her lips, in what looked like slow motion. She arched one perfectly shaped eyebrow at times, looking thoughtful at the bakes and making notes. I felt as if I was at a job interview and someone was dissecting my CV. Finally, she swallowed and patted her lips with the napkin I had provided. "These are amazing, darling. How long have you been baking?"

"Nearly four weeks."

"I thought you were about to say years. Sweetie, you're a natural. I'll do a piece on you if you like, for the paper?"

"Would you?"

"Absolutely. I feel as if I've discovered you."

My phone dinged with a text.

"Don't mind me, darling," said Izzy pointing at the phone on the table.

I looked at the screen it was from an unknown number. I opened the text.

It's bring a friend day at the gym tomorrow. Meet you at eight a.m. at the treadmills. Tell reception you're my guest and they will direct you. H

He must have got my number from Annie. The

gym was not my scene but at least it was a public place, I needed to see H again to find out more information, and after hearing what Wendy had to say – maybe it wasn't such a good idea to meet him again in private.

"Anything exciting?"

"H has invited me to the gym."

I noticed Izzy's eyes narrow but she continued to smile. "Oh. I see."

"I'm not really into the gym. Are you a member?" I asked.

"Yes, twice a week."

I needed to somehow direct the subject around to H and Zoe. I wondered how to approach it.

"So, tell me," said Izzy. "What's this all about, then? The visions you've been having about poor Zoe. I'm fascinated."

As much as I hated talking about the supernatural experiences, I was pleased to have a way into the topic. "Pretty creepy, actually. I've never believed in ghosts. I don't know what to think about it all. But it's made me curious about Zoe and what happened to her. But I know it's painful for everyone to think about it. It must have been such an awful time for you all."

Izzy sat back in her seat and crossed one long leg over another. "Indeed it was."

"So I take it you were close with Zoe? Did she have any enemies?" *Okay not so subtle.* I really needed to get my game on.

"Zoe was an angel, a really gentle soul. We were friends before college, we also went to school together. I loved spending time with her. I loved her to the core." Izzy lowered her eyes.

I felt a bit guilty asking but I had to move the conversation on. "H was pretty heartbroken by it all, then?"

"I didn't get the impression Zoe was that into him at the time – I think she was confused. H however, was quite obsessed with her."

"Obsessed?" I swallowed. *Do I really want to meet H at the gym?*

"Well, he's one of those guys that if he's into something, he's really into it. You know – when he gets his teeth into something, darling, he won't let go. It works well with his job. He's often caught the bad guy long after others have given up. But I'm sure H wouldn't have hurt Zoe. He was pretty cut up, I'm just saying – I'm not sure it was true love on Zoe's part. We discussed it, I ..." Izzy took a sip of tea. "It's all in the past now. I so wish our friendship wasn't cut short."

Annie had said there were tensions between H and Izzy. Maybe he'd thought she'd been interfering. I frowned.

"Darling, don't be put off by what I say. You and H have a clear attraction."

"What? Oh, no. I'm not dating him. He's not my type," I said, feeling heat rush to my face. "He couldn't get any further from my type if he tried."

"Is that so?" Izzy's face lit up and she took another bite of my Victoria sponge. I watched as she slowly ate it. "Divine."

"Do you think Zoe ran away?"

"I don't know what happened to her, no-one does. That's why the fact you've had these dreams is so fascinating. Because ..." Izzy paused and took a breath. "Some of us – we still need to find closure." She looked me straight in the eye. "If she's dead and speaking from the grave, you'll be able to find out what happened. Has Zoe said anything?" she said looking deeply into my eyes, like a python eyeing up its prey.

Oh dear. Izzy seemed to be turning this into an interrogation of me. I had planned it to be the other way around. I had to admit, I wasn't great at this amateur sleuth lark. "No, Zoe has said nothing to me," I lied. I didn't want to tell her that Zoe had started to speak to me – that she said. 'I would,' then disappeared.

Maybe Izzy was sussing me out to see what I knew because she was the killer? I gulped. There I was, new to Branden Bay and everyone I got close to ended up on my suspect list. This was not healthy. The sooner I got to the bottom of it, the better.

My palms began to sweat. There was a growing silence, so I needed to throw a question back.

"So, you and Zoe never fell out?" *Maybe not that direct.*

Izzy laughed. "Of course we fell out. We were

teenage girls. But deep down we both knew we loved ..." Izzy trailed off.

"What was her step-mother like?"

"Wendy?"

I nodded.

"My mother knows her quite well, they belong to the same society."

"The Branden Bay Ladies?"

"Yes, that's it. H had a fixation with Wendy, though. As is his way. He was always suspicious of her. As were a lot of people around here."

That tied in with what Wendy had said about H. I felt that some of the pieces were slotting together but nothing was telling me what had actually happened.

"Although Wendy was always sweet to me when I visited Zoe at the house. She often stops to chat, if I see her about town. Zoe used to moan about her every now and again but what sixteen-year-old doesn't have problems with their parents? I definitely did. So, Becky, what exactly have you seen and heard from the other side?"

Back to me again, then? This conversation was turning into a game of tennis. I felt fluff on my legs and glanced down to see Constance staring up at me. She meowed and I felt a strong need to keep my paranormal experiences close to my chest. "Not much. I've only seen shadows."

"How do you plan to move forward with your gift?" Izzy scribbled into her notebook.

"Lynn seems to want me to develop it but I've heard mixed reviews about the spiritualist church." I nodded towards the opening in my back-garden wall.

Izzy looked thoughtful. "They're not popular with everyone, darling. And, of course, Lynn was friends with Zoe's Dad and like an aunt to Zoe when we were little."

That fitted in with what Jeff said.

"From what Zoe said at the time, Lynn never got along with Wendy."

Constance jumped on my lap and I stroked her head. "Both seemed to know my Grandma."

"Everyone knew your Grandma, darling. My mother said that while Constance was very private, she was always at events in the town. There was talk that she had the gift, too."

Seemed like Izzy had been asking her mother for all sorts of information. "Well, the whole paranormal thing scares me. I don't intend to explore it."

Izzy's eyebrows rose and she nodded before scribbling on her pad again. "Interesting."

I frowned, hoping her notes were all food related. I needed to change the subject and bat the ball back into her side of the court. "At dinner the other evening – you guys seemed really close."

"We are. After Zoe disappeared, things got tense between us. You know what it's like, everyone feels their loss is greater. We went a year or so without contact. I'd got a modelling contract and was away an awful lot. We all made different friendship groups. Then after a couple of years, we came back together again. It's been nine years now and we've all moved on." She raised her eyebrows. "That is until you had this sighting." She rose to her feet. "It's brought everything back."

"I'm sorry."

"You've nothing to apologise for, sweetie. And I've really enjoyed spending time with you. I'm so excited about the charity tea." She smiled. "And seeing your adorable kitty again," she said, sweeping down to pet Constance. "Gorgeous."

Constance lifted her head and purred like a feline princess.

At the front door we shared a double air kiss.

"You'd better get your bake on, honey." Izzy smiled at me fluttering her long lashes. "And if you have any more of those weird dreams, be sure to tell me all about it. You have my number."

Constance followed Izzy down the path then jumped on the wall. I followed her and leaned on the wall, watching the world go by for a while. I felt there was something Izzy was keeping from me. She seemed to be asking me way too many questions and I wished I knew what was going on behind those blue eyes.

Back in the house, I picked up my mobile and texted H to let him know I would meet him at the gym the following day. I needed to view him in this new light – as obsessive – to see if he could possibly fit into Wendy's description of him. The truth was hidden somewhere and I needed to find it.

CHAPTER 15

I picked up a carrier bag containing a towel, toiletries, shorts and a T-shirt and carried them to my tote bag. I wore a snazzy gym outfit I'd bought from Branden Bay's sportswear shop late the previous afternoon. I didn't fancy another outing in the glitzy trainers. My finances wouldn't allow me to stretch to a sports bag. After all, even if I liked the gym, I would be unable to afford the membership fee until I found myself work. As I reached for my tote bag, I noticed Constance curled up inside.

"Come on, Connie cat." I lifted her out. "Pets aren't allowed in the gym," I said as I put her to the side. She meowed at me as I filled the bag. "I still need to get you one of those proper pet carriers." I'd been too busy to visit the pet shop. "And a brush to groom you."

After leaving the house, I walked a large stretch of

the bay until I reached the end where the road swept up the hill. Part way up, Millars hotel and Leisure club sat. I wondered whether I would gain more clues on the case of missing Zoe. *Listen to you. Case?* I knew I was out of my depth.

The gym was on the lower ground floor. H told me to give his name at reception and he'd see me by the treadmills. As I reached the reception, a guy stood there, leafing through papers. He wore a T-shirt emblazoned with the Millars' logo. I removed the tote bag from my shoulder. I felt tired from the short walk up the cliff base and didn't know how I would survive a full workout. "Hi, I'm here for bring-a-friend-day?" I asked with a breathless voice.

He frowned. "Bring-a-friend?"

Obviously new to the job. "I'm the guest of Detective Blake." Goodness knows why I gave his work title. I guess it was because 'H' could refer to a lot of people who may have a name which began with that letter. *I could be the friend of a Helen or a Hubert.* They may not have known his name was Henry. Indeed, he hadn't even told me his name himself, I'd gleaned that from Wendy.

"You're Becky?" The guy looked surprised.

"That's me."

"The changing rooms are there." He pointed to a door with a silhouette of a woman on it. "You'll need this for the locker." He handed me a smooth silver token. "The facilities are signposted from inside. I'm Mike and if you have any problems, just ask."

"Thanks, Mike," I said, heaving my bag up from the floor.

After stuffing the locker with my belongings, I looked around the changing rooms. *Very swish.* The colour scheme was white and aquamarine and there was an invigorating aroma of zesty essential oils. *I miss the spas of London.* I tied my hair up as I looked at my reflection in front of the mirror. Firstly, I pulled it into a pony tail. *Hmm too much face, especially when I start getting hot and crimson.* I pulled a few tendrils down to cover my cheeks. I shook my head. *Not a good look.* I pulled the tie out of my hair and shoved it into the little zipped pocket in the back of my new work-out leggings. I picked up my water bottle and the small towel I'd brought to mop up my sweat – not that I was planning on working out that hard but it was listed on the 'what to bring' section of the Millars' website. I followed the sign that said, 'Gym'.

The door opened to reveal a sea of machines. One red-faced guy sat at a contraption, pulling his arms back and forth as metal slid against metal, teamed with his intermittent puffs and grunts, it sounded like a steam train climbing a hill. He stopped and let out a groan.

People do this for fun? I shook my head. As I rounded the corner, I saw H. He was easy to spot amongst the sweaty bodies. Tall, broad and cool looking. He stood with reception Mike. I was just about to call out when I heard him talking. I stepped back behind a machine with some sort of pully thing hanging off it.

"So what's all this 'bring-a-friend-day' about?" Mike asked.

I heard H laugh. "I wanted an excuse to ask her here."

Oh? Like that is it?

"Well she's arrived. I have to say I'm a bit shocked, mate," said Mike.

"What about?" H sounded surprised.

"She's not your usual type. She's short. She's got red hair and the colour of her skin looks like she's lived in a cave her whole life."

Blooming cheek. I put my free hand on my hip. So what if I wear factor fifty even on a rainy day? *I like to look after my skin, mate.* It wasn't my fault that I burnt to a crisp on the mildest of sunny days. I was taking a dislike to this Mike and contemplated stepping from behind the machine and giving him a piece of my mind.

"Well, there's something about her I like," said H. His voice sounded lower.

"Like what, exactly?" said Mike.

I started flexing my free hand – not that I'd hit anyone before but this Mike guy was pushing it.

"I just feel attracted to her," said H.

Uh oh.

"Not in a wham-bam-thank-you-mam way," he continued.

Thank goodness for that. I didn't want H to think this was some sort of date. It wasn't. I was here in my capacity as detective. I shook my head, who was I kidding. *Detective?*

"I feel like I want to protect her. Look after her."

Great. Having heard Wendy and Izzy describing him as an obsessive it looked like I might have a problem on my hands.

Mike laughed. "I don't believe this. You've gone soft."

"And she *is* attractive, not sure what you're on about, Mike."

"Hey, I never said she wasn't attractive. She's gorgeous. A classy girl. A real natural beauty."

Hmm. Mike wasn't so bad after all.

"I'm just saying, H, she's not a five foot ten gym bunny with a spray tan. As I said – not your usual type."

"I never said she was my date. She's new to the bay and I'm looking out for her."

I stood back against the wall, puffing out. That was good to know.

"But you have a point, maybe I need to look further than this place for future girlfriends." H gave a low throaty laugh. I felt a shiver up my back. *Is that Millars' ghost?* I looked around for any lurking shadows – there were none.

"I'd better get back out front," said Mike.

I breathed in and put my head down as he passed. I stared at my water bottle as if checking the ingredients (there was just one). I saw a pair of gym shoes stop. I looked slowly up a pair of dark, hairy legs to Mike's face and gave him a small wave.

"Hi," I whispered.

He gave a short laugh and thumbed in H's direction. "Did you hear all of that?"

I pulled a wide-mouth-frog smile and nodded.

"I won't tell." He winked at me. "And maybe me and you can get a drink sometime?"

I gave a quiet, yet nervous, laugh.

H TOOK me on a tour of the gym and showed me how the machines worked. It had been a relatively pain-free experience. He even suggested I walked on the treadmill as he had noted running was not my thing. I also had a stint on the cross-trainer, ten minutes on the rower and finished with a session on the bike. He left me alone a lot of the time which was great, as far as my personal space was concerned. But not much use for trying to gather information from him. So when he asked me to join him for coffee and a bacon butty in Millars' sea-view bar, I said yes. I showered, then in the café, sat munching the poshest bacon sarnie I'd ever had. It was an open sandwich with rindless bacon and a leaf of cos lettuce with green and red tomato slices and a fancy drizzle of Millars' own recipe brown sauce. We shared a cafetiere of Brazilian coffee.

"It's idyllic, isn't it?" I said, looking out at the sea view from our window table.

"It's what draws the day trippers." He took a sip of coffee. "What's the verdict? Are you going to join the gym?"

"I might. But the fees are a bit hefty."

"True, I get a reduction through work. I'll see if I can wangle a discount for you." He smiled in a soft brown-eyed way.

"I love the look of the pool." *And they have a full spa with hair salon.* "Certainly, worth considering, but only when I've got a job."

"Of course. How's the search going?"

It wasn't, was it? Because I was spending all of my time trying to find out about Zoe and planning the afternoon tea. "I'm still looking – no interviews yet. I'm planning an afternoon tea this coming Saturday for charity and hope to use it for networking."

"Maybe I'll pop by." He smiled again.

I felt a shiver run up my body and looked around. *Not again.* "So how was work yesterday? Any good cases?" I thought I'd turn the subject to his job before I casually asked for details about the case of his missing girlfriend.

"Job's going great but nothing I can discuss with you, I'm afraid."

Looks like I thrashed it out around the gym for nothing.

I needed to press him further. "With Zoe's step-mother moving away, don't you feel like looking through the files at work?"

"I've been through them," he said. "Although I shouldn't have – so keep that to yourself. There were no leads. Nothing to go on because no-one was looking for her. And as I said, they decided she'd left of her own accord."

"So they never questioned anyone?" I dropped in, casually sipping my coffee and avoiding eye contact.

"Well, they hauled me in."

"Really?" *So it's true, he was the prime suspect.*

"They were a bit heavy-handed, spouting off the stats that the usual killer is the boyfriend."

"Nooo," I said summoning a surprised expression.

"Yep. Not a great time. It was Wendy, that's Zoe's step-mother, who pointed the finger at me."

"Really?" I wondered whether that was true or not. She said he had pointed the finger at her. "So how did Zoe get on with Wendy?"

"She didn't."

"Why's that?"

"She said Wendy monopolised Thomas. Wendy wanted him all for herself – that's what Zoe said. She bossed Zoe around. Dishing out the rules."

"Sometimes boundaries are good with teenagers," I said, remembering my parents laying down the law with me. "What were the rules she didn't like?"

"I can't remember the details, just that Wendy seemed to be a bit of a control freak."

"Did you spend much time with them as a family?"

H shook his head. "We were only together for about eight months and we spent most of our time out or at mine. She liked to get away from her home life."

I felt there was nothing more I was going to get out of H regarding Wendy – he didn't seem to know her other than what Zoe had told him. And as Izzy pointed out – a lot of teenager's rebel against their parents. I decided to turn the conversation to Izzy.

"It must have been awful for all of you, especially Izzy, she seemed really fond of Zoe."

H stood up. "She was definitely that. I'd better get going. Great seeing you again, Becky."

Well, that told me. He clearly wasn't going to give me any more information. than that which I already knew.

"I've really enjoyed this morning," he said. "Hopefully see you soon?"

I nodded but didn't make any suggestion of a follow up.

"I'll definitely see you on Saturday at the afternoon tea," he said.

As I watched him walk away, I felt a pang of loneliness. I looked out of the window and reached into my bag for my smartphone and updated my case notes. I felt as if I was getting nowhere. I had absolutely nothing concrete. How was I going to find out what happened to Zoe? All I had was a wishy-washy nothing. I shook my head. I was none the wiser. Instead of eliminating people, all I seemed to do was add more suspects to my list.

I decided to push away all thoughts of ghosts and death and concentrate on the charity afternoon tea.

CHAPTER 16

*T*he day of the charity afternoon tea had arrived. I'd been baking in my kitchen since dawn. It was becoming the norm, to see the ghost of Thomas walking through my house. Yet it never failed to scare me. I trembled with static every time his shadowy form appeared. I'd taken to carrying Constance around the house with me, like a comforter.

The only person remaining on my list to interview about the case, was Lynn. I felt embarrassed at myself for even trying to find out what happened to Zoe, but still felt a strong push to continue and Thomas's ghosts was a constant reminder. Lynn was due to help me carry the tables through the door at the end of my garden at 10 o'clock. This would be the perfect opportunity to ask her questions.

I washed my hands, removed my apron and pushed the back door wide open. I walked up the lawn, passing Constance who sat under the apple tree on Grandma's bench. She followed me with her gaze as I approached the door in the back wall. As I walked through, I found Lynn leaning against the hut wall with her face to the sun, her bushy hair glinting.

"Lovely day," she said. "You'll be able to have your doors open. Have you thought about putting a table out on the front patio?"

"I wasn't planning to, but I do have a nice little café-style table and chairs in my snug I could use."

"Yes, do. Now, let's get those tables through."

As we went back and forth, it was difficult to engage in conversation. We took a rest, having carried three of the tables through.

"Thanks for lending me these. I really appreciate it. Would you like to try the tea I've selected for today?"

"Thanks, lovey," she said and followed me to the kitchen.

"Izzy helped me choose it. You know, Annie's friend?"

"Oh yes, she used to play with Zoe when she was little and of course, she's famous locally for her modelling."

Maybe I needed to go straight for details on suspects higher up my list.

"Wendy's coming today, from the Ladies Society."

Lynn raised her eyebrows. "Wendy Palmer?"

"Yes. What do you think of her?" I said as I filled the tea pot.

Lynn pursed her lips. "We were never friends, not even when she was with Thomas. She kept a tight leash on that man."

"Thomas, as in Zoe's dad?"

"Yes. I was long-term friends with him. We were together at one stage shortly after his first wife died, although that didn't work out. We had so much history we were more like family. I guess that's why I put pressure on you when you told me about the reference to Zoe. Thomas could be the shadow you're seeing."

She was right there but I didn't want to confirm or deny.

"I never thought he'd absconded," she said. "Especially leaving Zoe and Wendy in a weak financial position. He was an honourable man with a clear sense of right and wrong." She blinked rapidly. "He liked to take chances, loved an adventure. He was a risk taker but he was a man of his word." She pushed her hair back off her face. "After a year or so, I tried to contact him myself, to see if he'd died. But I had no success. But you can't call up everyone, it doesn't work like that …"

"Were you on good terms when he went missing?" I asked.

"Let's get the last table in, while the tea's brewing. We haven't really got time for gossip," she said giving me the impression that she thought I was being nosey. Yes, I was trying to find out the details but it wasn't because I was a gossip. I wanted to help Thomas and

Zoe. But I couldn't tell her that. I sighed. How on earth would I be able to establish what happened when everyone kept everything so close to their chests?

"Hey, lovey, don't frown," said Lynn. "Today's your special day. Now get yourself ready and I'll help set everything up."

I smiled at Lynn. When she wasn't trying to recruit me to her church, she could be really kind. She was right. I needed to get on, I had seventy-five guests coming over and three sittings. *Seventy-five.* I rushed up the stairs.

THE GLASS DOORS in the bay window to the front of the house were wide open and, as Lynn had suggested, I placed my round, cafe-style table and four chairs on the front patio. Floral cloths adorned the tables, over which I'd placed smaller white cloths that I intended to change between services. I had three sessions booked. Firstly, I had Annie and her friends plus Lynn's friends from the church. The second sitting was for Wendy with the Branden Bay Ladies society and the last was filled with those who had contacted me after the leaflet drop.

Annie arrived through the open front glass doors. "Oh Becky, it looks lush – like a real cafe."

"I feel frazzled," I said, laughing.

"Well you look the proper hostess, standing there in your pretty outfit."

I glanced down at my top and skirt, another outfit I'd lifted from Grandma's wardrobe. "I'm set to make a tidy sum for the hospice."

"I can't wait, I've got the day off work. So order me around and I'll do whatever I can."

"Thanks, Annie." I felt a warmth inside. It was lovely having her help. One thing I was sure of, Annie was not on my suspect list.

She followed me to the kitchen, where Lynn was buttering freshly sliced bread which I'd had delivered from the bakery. I hadn't quite got to grips with bread baking myself.

"Thanks Lynn." I realised that, without their help, I would have been stressed and up to my elbows in butter.

I turned to Annie. "Lynn's making up the sandwiches. All the cakes are baked – it's just a case of assembling everything on the cake stands." I'd managed to find a couple in the local second-hand shop and a few cheap one's from the budget store.

"I can manage that," said Annie.

"Great. I've drawn a plan of what goes where. I'll do the waitressing." I smiled as I handed over the printed sheet with the details.

I breathed out as the first sitting guests were seated and the afternoon teas had been distributed. I surveyed the room. There were twenty-five people seated, with three cake stands on each of the large tables. The room was filled with chatter and the clanging of spoons against china, which filled me with tingles – and not the spooky kind.

I felt a rush of pride and a lump appeared in my throat. *I wish Grandma was here to see this.* I felt the familiar rub against my legs of Constance. She was a real hit with the customers and her coat was exceptionally neat since I'd groomed her first thing. The pet store had brushes especially for long coats and I'd at last picked her up a pet bag.

I moved through the tables and Constance followed me out front. I nodded at the guests sitting outside and she jumped onto the wall and purred as I stroked her. I looked back inside my house. It looked like a real café.

"You know what, Connie cat? I feel like I've fully arrived in Branden Bay." I blinked away a tear. "I'd better get back inside and mingle," I said. She lifted her head and I gave her a quick rub under her chin.

Lynn and Annie had both come through and were seated with their friends, pouring out teas. I noticed a few of the people from the tables look at me and smile, they probably all knew the gossip about me being the only person able to make contact with Zoe Palmer. I sighed; I knew the only way I was going to get any more information was to connect again. But I would worry about that later, I wanted to enjoy the day. I heard someone call my name and turned and saw Izzy sitting with a friend, as she snapped pictures with her phone. She waved me over.

"Darling, this is amazing. It's better than Millars." Izzy had her notebook out. She turned to her friend. "This is Maya."

A smart-looking Maya wore a black shirt and white trousers. She smiled showing bright teeth "It's totally sick. Could I use your restroom?"

"Of course." I pointed in the right direction. "Through that door." Hoping very much that 'sick' meant 'good' and had no links whatsoever with nausea.

I sat down and Izzy smiled at me. "Have you had any more dreams?"

Not this again. "No."

"So where did you see first the shadow? Was it in this room?" She scanned the lounge and snapped a couple of pictures.

I shook my head. "No. Mainly in my bedroom and the kitchen."

"In the kitchen?" She looked at the door.

"Yes, sitting at the table."

"I see. What did he say again?"

I sighed. "I told you, he didn't say anything." Was she trying to trip me up, by asking me the same questions? Or was she being nosey? It was difficult to tell.

"Do you think we should all get together and have a seance?" She looked across to Lynn's friends.

I shuddered. "No, Izzy. I've already said I'm not into

that sort of thing. Anyway, I have to get back to my hostess duties." I was getting tired of this attention from Izzy and a part of me suspected that she might be sounding me out, to see if I knew more than I was letting on. She was beginning to look guilty. I felt as if she was hiding something from me.

Annie waved me over. "You should think about opening as a café."

I laughed as I walked over to the table she was sitting at. "This is friends over for tea and cake, a bit different to running a business with staff and what have you."

"But all you need is one of those shiny coffee machines and it could be a café," said Annie.

I leaned on the back of her chair and looked over to the far wall, *I guess I could stick a machine there.* "But they're probably too expensive and I have no funds."

"This used to be a café," said Mrs Jessup, my elderly neighbour sitting at the table to my right. "When I was a little girl I came here a lot."

"Really – it was a café?" I asked looking around the room.

She nodded and pointed to the front. "Yes, long before your granny moved in. That's why you have a glass door there."

I looked to the bay window, then around the room. It did look as if the room was made for a cafe. It had always felt empty and lonely, but right then it felt like it had a life.

"Go on, open a café. Everyone's raving about your cakes and you've taken loads of money. This is only the first sitting," said Annie.

Constance had returned into the room and jumped onto Annie's lap and sniffed at the sandwich on her plate.

"No, you don't, Connie cat," I scolded.

"I don't mind," said Annie.

"Maybe not, but the next customer might." I ruffled the fur on Constance's head. "You can spend the rest of the time in the snug, Missy." I picked her up and she meowed in protest as I put her out back.

The first sitting was soon up and I rang a bell announcing the end of service. A queue of Branden Bay Ladies was already forming along Beach Road. Annie and Lynn kept things going in the kitchen, which was good – I didn't want an awkward moment with Wendy. They were kept busy washing up the first set of crockery so that it was ready for the third sitting. Wendy was out front collecting the money. All I had to do was plonk the cake stands and tea pots on the tables.

After half an hour, Wendy looked animated as she approached me. "This is amazing, Becky. Everyone's having so much fun." She handed me a large envelope holding the money taken.

"Wow, thanks, Wendy."

"The thanks goes to you. You've made this happen." She lifted a handkerchief to her eyes. "I feel like a part of the town again. I'm rethinking my move. Yes, I'll sell the house, it's too big." She smiled at me. "But this past week, I've felt like a new person. Like I've found family." She rubbed my arm. "One of the sea-facing apartments is up for sale just along from here. I may consider that."

"That's lovely. You do a lot for your group and I'm sure everyone loves and appreciates you. They'd miss you if you moved away." I smiled back at her. "I'm glad I've met you, too." And I meant it.

Her eyes glassed over. "Bless you, Rebecca. You're a breath of fresh air." She wiped her eyes and looked over my shoulder. "I see you have a couple of helpers in?"

"Er, yes," I said as my face heated up. "I asked Lynn if I could borrow some of the tables from the hut and she's out there with her friend, Annie."

I knew Wendy warned me off Lynn and I didn't have the time now to tell the whole story about Lynn coming over and me going to dinner at Annie's. I would explain – but I couldn't do at that moment, especially not with them being there.

Wendy smiled and went back to her mingling and I returned to the kitchen. Lynn looked frazzled and flushed as they both sat down to drink tea.

"I'm enjoying this so much. You have to open a café," said Annie.

I laughed. "It's quite fun, isn't it? But I'm sure the novelty would soon wear off."

Lynn glanced at me and smiled. I wondered what she'd seen in her crystal ball – not that I knew whether she used one. I hadn't asked Lynn at all about her own gift.

"We're only half-way through, remember?" I said to Annie. "In another hour and a half you'll probably feel differently."

I rang the bell to signify the end of the second service and received a round of applause from the Branden Bay Ladies who also complimented me individually and asked for recipes as they left. They were excited about me joining their group.

Wendy did not leave until the last set of customers were seated and served. I stood with her outside at the front wall.

"I wondered whether you'd like to join me for a traditional Sunday lunch tomorrow?" she asked.

"I'd love to, especially as I've cooked for the masses today," I said, laughing.

"One o'clock?"

"Great, see you tomorrow."

Wendy gave me a hug and then left. I turned and saw H approaching. I smiled but he frowned.

"What do you think you're playing at?" His eyes were dark.

My shackles went up immediately. "What do you mean?"

"Up close with Wendy Palmer. Are you stupid?"

"No, H, I'm not stupid. But you are very rude."

"I warned you about her."

"I've not seen any evidence of her being a murder-er." I crossed my arms. "Do you think that maybe you've been barking up the wrong tree?" Which was apt because he looked like a Rottweiler ready to pounce.

"She's evil," he growled.

"So you say. The poor woman has had her name dragged through the mud for years." I nodded towards the table out front with a group of young women who were looking in our direction. "And keep your voice down, please."

He lowered his voice. "Look I know in here," he thumped his chest, "that she had something to do with Zoe going missing. You've got to believe me."

I shook my head. "I don't want to talk about this right now."

"Promise me you won't see her again without speaking to me first."

I nodded with my fingers crossed behind my back. I didn't want to have a heated discussion in front of paying guests. H strode away, clearly deciding he didn't want to stay for tea and scones.

I shivered and went in to collect payments from the last sitting. I puffed out a huge sigh. It seemed that Izzy and Wendy were both right. H was obsessive and he had moved right to the very top of my suspects list.

CHAPTER 17

*B*y six o'clock, seventy-five people had been fed and they all appeared to have left my house happy. The washing-up was done and it had been the longest day of my entire life. After the last sitting, some visitors bought takeaway cakes and I sold a few to passers-by who thought a new café had opened. I felt a flutter of excitement in my chest. *Could I open a café?*

I flopped down on the sofa in the snug and Constance jumped onto my lap purring. I always felt better about things when she was close. And I was still troubled by H's visit. I looked into her bright green eyes as I scratched underneath her chin.

My phone dinged with a text. It was Jeff. I opened it.

Sorry about the other night. If you want to talk, I'm here.

I studied the text. I certainly had unfinished business. I needed to get back on the case. Every evening I dreaded the onset of nightfall – knowing that Thomas would be appearing in his shadowy form. The only way forward was to get in touch with Zoe because she was able to speak, whereas Thomas appeared unable to say a word. As much as Jeff was like a little boy playing with dangerous toys, I could do with his help to get this well and truly wrapped up, then I could get on with my life. *Maybe open the café.* With that new goal I felt propelled into action.

"Should I use Jeff again?" I asked Constance. She jumped up and meowed at the door. I rose to let her out. Maybe I needed to consider a pet door. She bolted up the garden to the back gate and waited patiently. There was no way I was going to start opening doors for her. *What's she like?* I grinned. "You'll have to jump over this time," I called to her.

I texted Jeff and invited him over. Adrenaline kept my tiredness at bay.

HALF AN HOUR later the bell rang and I opened the door. "Hi Jeff."

"Er, hi," he said looking at me, then down at his hands. "I'm sorry about what happened the other night." He seemed genuinely upset.

I stepped to one side. "Come in. I can't stand on my feet for much longer, I've been on them all day."

Sitting at the kitchen table, we ate ugly cakes: those that I was not prepared to serve. I realised I hadn't eaten myself all day and dived into the pile. I ate a lop-sided fruit scone with a thick spreading of butter. Jeff grabbed a muffin with a crater in the middle. Constance, back from the garden, sat on a chair watching Jeff as he chewed.

"Here's the thing," I said. "I get the feeling that unless I find Zoe, the shadow of Thomas will haunt me forever."

"Is he still here?" Jeff asked looking around the room.

I saw movement in the corner of my vision and nodded, shivering as static tapped at my neck. Constance hissed at the shadow, then directed an equally grumpy hiss at Jeff.

"Wish I could see ghosts without the gear," Jeff said.

"I wish I didn't. That's life, I guess," I sighed.

"Have you got a plan?" Jeff asked.

"I've been trying to solve the mystery of Zoe's disappearance without resorting to paranormal measures – using detecting skills."

"What detecting skills do you have?"

"None. That's the problem – I'm useless at it. But I've been investigating anyway."

"You're joking right? No-one else in the town managed that and you've only been here a few weeks."

I picked up my mobile phone to retrieve my notes. "I've interviewed all of my main suspects."

"Like who?"

"Her step-mother, Wendy; Izzy; Lynn, and her boyfriend Henry, otherwise known as H."

"What? You interviewed a copper?"

"I've interviewed all of them, yes. But I've got nowhere." I shook my head. "I found literally zero information."

"What nothing?"

I referred to my phone. "I've been taking notes." I paused. "Lynn has been on my case to develop my gift but has since admitted she also wants to find out more about Zoe."

"Told you."

"Indeed, she admitted to her history with Thomas but was very cagey when I pursued that line of enquiry and didn't want to discuss it with me in any detail."

"She wouldn't, would she?" Jeff picked up a rather flat lemon cup cake.

"Then there's Izzy. She had an almighty row with Zoe just before she went missing. She was jealous of Zoe's relationship with H, but it seems she was definitely not interested in H herself. She didn't say, but I'm guessing she was in love with Zoe herself."

"Right," Jeff said.

"And she's beyond nosey, constantly asking me about the ghost."

"Sounds like she might be thinking she's going to get found out."

"Exactly what I wondered – although Constance loves her."

"Constance?"

"My cat."

Constance hissed at Jeff again.

"Well the cat doesn't seem to like me very much – hope you're not adding my name to your list of suspects?"

I laughed. "I might have done if you hadn't been a little kid when Zoe went missing." I wondered how old Jeff was. I assumed he was about twenty, which would have made him eleven at the time. "I wonder if Thomas died at the same time as Zoe, or whether he passed away since? It's all so complicated."

"What about Zoe's boyfriend?"

"He was prime suspect at the time Zoe went missing – due to the stats showing that the boyfriend usually is the killer."

"We're talking about the copper here?"

"Yes, and he's apparently obsessive and controlling." I looked up from my phone. "And he's been very off with me. Telling me who I should and shouldn't mix with."

"But he's police. They like to boss people around. Who's he saying you shouldn't see?"

"Wendy Palmer."

Jeff gave a short laugh. "Maybe he's got a point. My Mum reckons she done it."

"She probably listens to local gossip and didn't your Mum tell you to steer clear of me?"

"True." Jeff rubbed his scrappy beard. "And what was H's motive?"

"Lovers tiff gone wrong?" I grabbed a lemon cupcake for myself. They were totally yummy. "Wendy is sure that H is responsible for her bad reputation and the gossip that was spread about her. She said it was a smokescreen."

"Deflecting the attention from himself?" Jeff continued to stroke his hairy chin. "Interesting."

"Maybe. Wendy appears genuinely upset when she speaks about it. She tears up."

"That could be guilt." Jeff took a bite of cake and chewed thoughtfully. "What are your notes on her?"

"H said that Zoe hated Wendy and referred to her as the step-witch. That she came between her and her father. Wendy has admitted that she fell out with Thomas because he lost her money on a deal gone bad – she's not denying that or pretending all was well between them."

"What evidence have you got from your paranormal activity?"

"As you know, we assume it was the ghost of Thomas who gave us the message to find Zoe and ..." I hesitated.

"What?"

"When you were out looking for your phone after things went mad here, I saw Zoe and I asked her where she was and she started to speak but you came back in and she disappeared."

Jeff frowned. "You saw her and she spoke? You never told me that. What did she say?"

"She said 'I would,' and then disappeared when you came in – cut off mid-sentence."

"What are we waiting for? Let's call her up now and get this thing sorted." Jeff stood up. "I'll get my gear out of the van."

I bit my lip. "That's what I wanted to talk about. I've been avoiding talking to the dead but I guess using my gift is the only way forward – I make a useless amateur sleuth." I yawned and shook my head. "I can't do it tonight, the events of the day are catching up with me."

"I'm working tomorrow, I've got a part-time job for the summer up at the big D.I.Y store at the retail park." said Jeff. "I'll come over tomorrow at about six after I finish."

After Jeff left, I climbed into bed with Constance by my side. If the ghost of Thomas was around, I wouldn't have noticed as I fell asleep as soon as my head touched the pillow.

The following day was sunny and after a spot of baking I spent the rest of the morning in the garden, sitting beneath Grandma's apple tree on her bench thinking long and hard about whether I should open a café. Constance chased a butterfly around the lawn and I smiled watching her, she seemed so young and carefree and made no effort to actually catch and eat the bug.

At twelve o'clock, I left my house for Wendy's. I was looking forward to a traditional roast. I walked up the hill towards Upper Ashcombe Road lugging my bag full of the rich, and rather heavy, fruit cake I'd baked that morning. Indeed, it still had not fully cooled. I panted as I reached the steep drive to her house. I looked back and Constance was still following me, meowing as I went. "You can't come in. Why did you follow? You'll have to wait outside," I said.

Constance sat down and fluffed out the fur on her chest in disapproval.

When I reached the house, Wendy was waiting for me at the door. She looked over my shoulder, frowning.

"Are you okay?" I asked.

"I think someone has been watching the house today."

I turned around. "Who?"

She shook her head. "I used to get stalked all the time after Zoe went missing. Maybe it's because I've got the house up for sale." She brushed her dark hair off her forehead. "It's bringing everything back to me, I'm probably being paranoid. But I hope Henry isn't watching me."

I hesitated. *Should I fess up now? Tell her I know him?* I could share with her that he'd been giving me a hard time as well. But I decided against it. I wanted to enjoy a stress-free lunch. I'd get back to the paranormal sleuthing once Jeff came over to mine after work. I'd ask Zoe – who did it? And hopefully the whole nightmare would be over.

Wendy turned back. "Don't look so concerned. I was probably imagining things." She smiled and I followed her into her home and through to the kitchen.

I pulled the cake box out of my bag. "I don't like to come empty-handed."

"How sweet of you. Pop it on the worktop. At least I've got you, Rebecca, I'm so pleased you walked into my life. Someone to trust."

I gulped. I wasn't exactly being completely honest with her.

We engaged in a tasty meal of roast beef with Yorkshire puddings, roasted parsnips and carrots with a thick delicious gravy.

Wendy patted her tummy. "I'm feeling lethargic after that big lunch. Do you fancy walking it off?" she asked. "There's a lovely spot on the other side of the hill, with views over Cormorant Cove. It's quite breathtaking." She looked at my cake. "Leave all your gubbins here, love. I'll pop a chunk of your cake and a flask in a backpack."

As WE LEFT THE HOUSE, I popped my mobile into my cardigan pocket in case I needed to text Jeff later to cancel our paranormal get-together. After all, I'd probably be tired after the walk. Static ripped up my back, so much so that it took my breath away. But I ignored it. I wanted one day – just one day – without ghosts and without being obsessed with missing bodies ... But that wasn't going to happen.

CHAPTER 18

*W*endy carried the small backpack over her shoulder and wore jeans and a T-shirt. She led me around the front of the house. I looked up at the imposing property.

"When will the sale go through?"

"Depends on the solicitors but the Abercrombie's are cash buyers, so not too long, I hope. It will be a while until they move in, though, Mrs Abercrombie wants to give birth first and she doesn't want to move in until the contractors have fully refurbished the place. Wendy looked at the house. "It's going to look beautiful," she said wistfully. She passed me. "This way, there are steps at the side of the property which run up to my garden with a gate to the woods."

I knew that, of course, because Stephen had shown me. But I didn't mention it, not wanting to remind her of my rude, uninvited entry into her property.

I was glad of the flat shoes I'd worn and wished I too was wearing jeans rather than a skirt and top. I pulled my cardigan around me as we walked into the shade. It wasn't as warm without the sun shining on me. The steps were quite overgrown.

"Be careful, hold onto the rail," said Wendy.

I was rather puffed when we reached the top but Wendy seemed to be taking it in her stride.

"Do you work out?" I asked her.

"I live on a hill. Walking down to the bay and back keeps me fit."

I heard a whimpering meow and looked behind to see Constance following us up.

"Connie," I called. "What are you doing up here?"

"Is that your cat again?"

"Yes, sorry."

"Oh well, the more the merrier."

At the top, we reached Wendy's garden. It was totally overgrown with a tired-looking summer house in the corner. At the back of the garden were a few trees, then a high stone wall with an iron gate in it.

"The views from here were amazing before the bushes grew. You could see right across to Wales and its famous rolling hills." She shook her head. "Such carefree days."

I could see the sadness in her eyes. Wendy turned and walked towards the gate. She pushed it and as it creaked open, I felt a slight shock of static.

Constance caught up with me and meowed.

"You don't have to follow us, if you don't like it. Wait here, we'll be back in a while."

Constance meowed again.

I bent down and she pawed at my wrist. "You're safer here." I went through the gate and closed it behind me. I didn't want her getting lost in the trees. Constance soon appeared on top of the wall then jumped down beside me. "If you insist on coming, stick close to me." I would have carried her but I was already puffed out.

Wendy beckoned me. "It's a bit of a trek, but well worth it."

I'd not been over to that section of the woods before. On the other side of Branden Hill was an unspoilt cove forming part of a nature reserve. I'd heard it was very beautiful and was looking forward to seeing it. The small, stony beach was known for its strong rip tide, so I had not visited the cove on foot. But seeing it from the hill would be ideal.

Wendy was not exaggerating when she'd said it was a bit of a trek. It wasn't the distance that was a problem but the terrain. A lot of it was overgrown and we had to squeeze through bushes which scratched my arms and legs. *No wonder this part is quiet* – there wasn't much evidence that many people visited. I wished I'd brought water. *I'm looking forward to drinking the tea Wendy's brought.*

Constance managed to keep up but I felt a seeping sickly feeling inside. Probably me worrying that I would lose her up there. Finally, we reached a clearing. In the middle was an old sign post with 'High Wood' written on it, in peeling red paint.

"High Wood?" Why was that repeating in my head? *High Wood.*

Wendy stopped and put her hands on her hips. "The Victorians used to come to this part for the views. It's known as High Wood to distinguish it from the main wood. There are a few works of art on display at the Town Hall depicting the cove from this angle. But I've never seen anyone here."

"It's an idyllic spot for a picnic," I said as I looked around me. All was silent apart from the rustling of leaves, distant seagulls and the sound of waves crashing on rocks far below.

Constance meowed again.

"You shouldn't have come if you don't like it," I said bending down and picking her up. Constance didn't purr as she usually did. She felt stiff. "Poor mite is scared to pieces," I said. I carried Constance as I followed Wendy who headed towards a large rock, set in front of a fantastic view over the cove. My eyes were drawn again to the red sign. *High Wood.* Where had I heard that before? I heard Zoe's voice in my mind. "*I would ...*". A slow-moving chill seeped into my veins as realisation dawned on me. *High wood* – not "*I would ...*"

I swallowed and Constance meowed as I clutched her tightly. My heart thudded in the way that it would if I was attached to a railway track as an express train approached.

"Is the cat alright?" called Wendy.

Constance began her long wailing noise. This heightened the feeling of fear inside my body. My skin was clammy and I shivered as cool air swept across it. *Think, quick, think.*

"Let's have our tea, then." Wendy sat on the rock which was flat. "Come and see, it's such a great view."

As I approached, Constance jumped down and scraped at the floor next to the rock with her paws, as if she was preparing to go to the toilet.

"Constance, not now," I said, picking her up to move her behind a bush. As I did so, I saw a grate in the floor. "Looks like there's a drain here. I wonder what that's for?" I said trying to keep my voice casual. Fighting the urge to run, I felt a jolt of static travel up my spine.

"Maybe to take rain water away. Now stop fussing with the cat. It can do its business where it pleases. It's a wood. Come and sit down, I want you to see the view."

I sat next to Wendy on the rock, my throat felt dry. Maybe my imagination was running away with me – again. *Calm down.*

"You look hot and sweaty dear. Here." Wendy passed me a towel. "Wipe yourself with this."

Taking a deep breath, I mopped my brow, face and neck. I was over-reacting. I shouldn't let my thoughts run away with me. I heard H's voice in my head. *Promise me you won't see her again without speaking to me first.* I took the plastic cup of tea from Wendy and took a gulp, my mouth was so dry. "What sort of tea is this?" I asked. It wasn't her usual Earl Grey.

"It was a sample sent with my order. I thought I'd try something different."

It had an odd tang to it. I felt tired and a touch woozy. As I glanced down, the cup became a blur. *Oh, no she's drugged me.* "I need to have a wee." I said. "I'll just go behind that bush."

I heard Wendy's voice behind me. "You carry on." She laughed. It sounded evil.

What have I done?

I made it to the bush with Constance at my side. I pulled out my mobile and texted Jeff. The screen appeared awash with water and it was difficult to concentrate. I hoped the phone's predictive text would help me out.

Zoe in High Wood. Wendy killer. Tell H. Help.

I pressed send then buried the phone in the leaves as I lay on my back. My legs and arms felt heavy, I heard Constance meowing at me as Wendy's blurry face came into my vision. I watched Constance leap at her. Wendy's leg rose and kicked my little cat, her furry body flung into the air like a rag doll. A distant kitty cry reached my ears. *No ...* I wanted to scream but was paralysed. Everything went black.

. . .

MY HEAD HURT. I opened my eyes. It was dark but I saw shafts of light coming from above. I couldn't breathe that well and wondered why until I registered that I had tape across my mouth and my hands were also stuck together behind my back. I lay on a damp floor of mulchy vegetation as a chill oozed into my body.

Where am I? Am I dreaming? I squinted. I could see a grate above my head, where the light came in. I saw a vision in my mind's eye of my precious Constance scraping at the grate and then flying through the air over the side of the cliff. I moaned, unable to speak. *Constance.* Tears filled my eyes. *Please, don't be dead.* It was then that I realise how much I'd really grown to love that ball of fluff – she'd become the closest thing to me.

I blinked rapidly unable to wipe away the tears. I counted slowly to ten and breathed in as deeply as I could through my nose to calm myself.

Static rippled through me and I looked to my side. A muffled scream shot through my nostrils as I came face to face with the ghost of Zoe, her head down, her silver bob glistening, her arms clutching her knees, just as I'd seen her in my house. She lifted her head with her black marble eyes staring at me. I filled my nostrils with dank air. I wanted to scream out loud, really loud. But all I could manage was another whimper. It was as if someone had stolen my breath. As I stared at her, Zoe's image started to flicker and fade, as it diminished, I saw what was there, in the physical world. A skeleton was slumped against the wall. I shut my eyes, shaking. I slowly reopened them and turned my gaze to the right where I saw another skeleton, much larger. I guessed it was Thomas.

Adrenaline coursed through my body. I tried to pull my hands apart, the tape began to free up. *Wendy must have done this in a rush.* After a few seconds it came off. I pulled at the tape on my face. It was so sticky that it took three goes until I ripped it off. *Ouch.* I rubbed my sore face, *that's worse than a top lip wax.* I scrambled up and jumped, trying to reach the grate to pull myself up, but it was way too high. Let's face it, if it had been too high for Thomas to reach, I had no chance. I looked down at the remains of father and daughter. Poor Zoe. No-one would ever know she was here, unless I got out.

I screamed. "Help! Somebody help me!"

I did that for a while then slumped to the ground. No one heard and no-one was coming. I put my head into my hands and sobbed. What an idiot I'd been. H was right. So much for me being an amateur sleuth. What would Grandma think? She'd left me such a large gift, a house and a new life and I'd thrown it all away. Now I would be left down a hole to rot. My parents – they'd be heart broken. I knew I wouldn't last long – I'd either die of hyperthermia or thirst. My only hope was that Jeff received my text message.

I cried myself to sleep, the drugs were probably still in my system.

. . .

I woke to the sound of a meow. *Constance? Still alive?* I pulled myself up and saw her tiny paw poking through the grate and I put my hand up, but I could not reach her. "Connie cat, I love you," I said feeling tears run down my cheeks. I shuddered, not sure if it was from the cold or shock.

Constance hissed and give a low growl. Her paw disappeared. I sensed danger and sat down. *Wendy's back.*

CHAPTER 19

I slapped the tape back on my mouth and put my hands behind my back. Hearing the grate move, I opened my eyes to a slit.

"Hope you enjoy your resting place, Rebecca. Seeing as you were so intent on finding Zoe. I knew what you were up to. You thought I was stupid, didn't you?" She paused. "I know you can hear me. Just like I knew you were checking me out. This is a small town and I know a lot of people. I saw that paranormal van outside your house. Gossip was that you'd had contact from Zoe. Became friends with Annie and Izzy did you? And then you turned up snooping in my house? Pretending you just happened to be passing, eh? Stupid girl. And then the icing on the cake, you were seen out with Henry ... I gave you every opportunity to be honest with me. But you lied. It's a shame because I really liked you, Rebecca. Just as I liked Zoe."

I remained silent. I didn't want to give her the satisfaction of acknowledging her – I didn't want her to feel significant or that she had power over me. I'd rather play dead.

"You're sneaky. You let me down, just like everyone else. Thomas lost my savings, the stupid idiotic man. He had to pay – he was going to leave me. I brought him up here to talk, he was just as quick as you to take a drink but it took me ages to get him in the hole. Big bulk of a man. And then Zoe, we could have had a nice, simple life together but she constantly whinged and whined about her father. I told her he had been useless and to forget all about him but she insisted on blaming me. Saying it was all my fault he left. The three of you – all idiots – all falling for the same trick."

She leaned back and a slither of light shone into the hole. I heard her voice again. "I'm just dropping off the things you left at the house. I don't want any evidence of you for that knucklehead police officer to find. And I found your phone in the bushes. Really cute, leaving it hidden, but they won't be able to track you here on the GPS. I drove it round to Cormorant Cove with the towel you wiped your sweaty DNA on and your shoes. Looks like you went for a paddle, Becky, and got caught in the rip tide. Shame." She laughed. "No-one will be looking for you anywhere other than the sea and they'll assume you're in a watery grave." She sighed loudly. "Not that anyone will miss you. Your life is as sad as mine."

No, I thought. *I've got lots to live for.*

Wendy lowered my tote bag into the hole and as she did, the shoulder strap hung down. I knew I only had one shot at it. I leaped up and yanked it. There was a piercing scream as Wendy fell onto the floor beside me to the sound of an almighty crack as she hit the uneven stone floor.

"My leg," she screamed. It was twisted beneath her. She moaned then fell silent.

It began to rain and droplets fell in the now open hole. A flash of lightening sent shards of light into the pit followed by a deep rumble of thunder. I listened to the patter, breathing in the aroma of the dank dark space.

There was no sign of Constance – maybe Wendy had kicked her away again – this time finishing her off. Tears filled my eyes as the light faded; I had no idea what the time was. Was it dark due to the clouds? Or was night falling? I looked at the walls – I would not be able to climb them. This must be some sort of bunker I guessed. My heart instantly lifted as I heard the meow of a cat.

"Constance."

I heard my name being called in the distance. "Becky." Was that H?

"Becky." Was that Annie?

"I sense she's this way," that was definitely Lynn.

I could also pick out Jeff's EMF meter bleeping like crazy.

I took a deep breath and screamed with all my might. "I'm down here."

Constance meowed in a long wail. I stood up, adrenalin coursed through my body and gave me the energy to jump and cry out.

I felt a hand grip my ankle. Wendy had woken. I fell to the floor as she pulled at my leg and scratched me. Constance meowed and wailed from above and then I saw her fly down.

It's difficult to remember what happened next, it was all a bit of a whirl. I saw a large person lower in and push me to one side then there was a scuffle. I felt the warm fluffy body of Constance against me. Wendy cried out as I heard the click of handcuffs.

Annie called down. "Becky. Becky are you okay?"

"Yes. I'm fine," I shouted. Although I was far from fine – I was alive.

I glanced over to H. The torch on his phone lit the space. He sat next to Wendy's limp body, staring at the two skeletons. He put his head in his hands as his body shook. He didn't make a sound but I knew he was sobbing.

I SAT up in the hospital bed the following morning, reading a copy of a glossy magazine which Izzy had brought in for me. She'd managed to blag her way in before visiting time. It was her way of apologising for not joining the search party in the woods the previous day. I had to admit, tracking through the woods didn't strike me as Izzy's type of thing.

She sat, animated as I described what had happened with me and Wendy down the hole. She apologised for telling me Wendy was a lovely person, and admitted that she was clearly not a great judge of character.

"You and me both," I said.

She rushed off not long after that, explaining that she had to get back to the newspaper office.

I shook my head, telling myself off for thinking Izzy might have been a killer. And Lynn and poor H. Paranoia had certainly set in since I'd moved to Branden Bay.

I looked up as I saw someone standing in the doorway. It was H.

I felt a blush fill my cheeks. I knew he was about to tell me off. I decided to get my apology in first.

"I'm sorry for not taking any notice of you, H. I was taken in by Wendy. It's just been such a confusing few weeks, what with seeing ghosts when I don't believe in them. To be honest, I thought I was going mad and that probably made me paranoid."

"I'm not here to have a go at you."

"Oh, okay."

"Although you won't be surprised if I suggest you leave the investigating to the police in future. You could have come to me, you know, to discuss your thoughts."

I didn't want to tell him he'd been my prime suspect. "Yeah, I'm sorry about that."

"Jeff filled me in. Although I have to say, I still don't believe in all that ghost nonsense."

"Well, I won't be getting involved in any of that again. I'm sure it was just a one-off." I leaned forward. "How's Constance, my cat?"

"She was with Annie last night and has been dropped back to your house today."

I sat back. "It was awful, watching Wendy kicking her over the edge of the cliff, I thought she was dead."

"It's not a sheer drop that side, but I reckon your cat spent at least one of its nine lives yesterday. You're lucky she was there. We may have missed you if we hadn't seen her by the pit. She's quite unique – like her owner." He walked into the room and passed me a large bar of chocolate. "I thought we were going to find you dead back there."

"So did I," I said smoothing down my hair, glad that I'd been able to grab a shower at the hospital. "What about Wendy?"

"She's in traction and under a heavy guard. With two counts of murder and one of attempted, she's unlikely to ever taste freedom again."

Looking at his grave expression, I remembered how upset he was in the hole. "I'm sorry I didn't take your advice."

"Look, it's not your fault. I was being too forceful. I know how I came across. I was acting like I was sixteen again. All the fear came flooding back. I pushed you away."

"So what now?" I asked

"We have to identify the ... the bones." H puffed out. "The DNA will be tested and the teeth will be checked against dental records. But we know the remains are of Zoe and Thomas because we found their passports in there, which Wendy no doubt threw in after them. We've cordoned off the area and forensics are in. We won't be able to move them for some time. I'm on my way back up there now, I just wanted to check on you."

"I'm fine, I have bruises on my shoulder and legs where I fell. Lucky, I landed on a pile of mulch eh? I'm hoping to be discharged soon."

"Annie will be picking you up, but it's going to take a while for you to recover. It can't have been nice, finding yourself in a hole like that, thinking it was the end. So don't rush it. I see it at work all the time, victims with delayed reactions."

I raised my eyebrows. "Bossing me about again?"

He ran a hand through his hair. "Sorry. Um ... I also wanted to ask you ..."

"Yes?"

"I wondered about food?"

"I've got plenty in – always keep some tins at home for an emergency."

"No, I mean, about us having food."

What's he on about? Us?

He shifted his feet. "Look. You don't have to if you don't want to. I don't want to put you under pressure."

"Oh." I remembered when we'd eaten over at Annie's she said they all met up once a month for food. *That's what he's on about.* "Oh, yes, sure. At my place?"

His eyes opened wider and I could clearly see the warm brown. "I'd like that." He smiled.

"Yes sorry, I remember now that your gang meets up once a month – so I guess it's my turn." I laughed.

"Well I – "

"I'll invite Annie and Izzy, it'll be a great way of me saying thanks to you guys."

H frowned. "Er, yeah, right. Okay. But –"

Lynn popped her head around the corner. "Okay to interrupt?"

"Yep. I'm off now." H nodded at me and left.

Lynn chuckled. "Not making it easy for him are you? I like your style. A man like that's not used to having to chase a girl."

I frowned at Lynn. "What are you talking about?"

"Him asking you out like that and you teasing him. I've been earwigging around the corner."

I shook my head. *What is she on?* "He wasn't asking me out on a date."

Lynn laughed. "If you say so, dear. So, how's the little mystery solver then?" She asked, passing me a bag of grapes.

"Hardly a mystery solver."

"Why do you say that?"

"I nearly got myself killed. I should have asked for your help, I guess."

"Sometimes in life we follow our instinct and that's what you did, lovey. And that's how you solved the mystery."

"But all I did was unwittingly make friends with a killer."

Lynn rubbed my hand. "Jeff's told me all about it. Zoe told you from the grave that she was in High Wood and you found her. How is that not solving the mystery?"

"Well ... I feel like I just fell in – literally and found the bodies."

"Nonsense. This whole town has tried to solve the disappearance of Zoe and Thomas for years. You came to town and within a few weeks you found the killer and their resting place."

"I guess if you put it like that ..."

"But remember, if you have any more problems with seeing people, I can show you how to manage it."

"Oh no, it definitely won't happen again," I said.

"We need to stick together, lovey."

"But I'm not like you. I wouldn't have a clue how to call up someone's dead relative and neither do I want to."

"I know that, Becky. Your gift is different to mine. I'm here for the living. I connect with them and help them contact the other side so they can come to terms with their loss."

"Exactly, that's not me. I'm not a medium."

"You on the other hand are here for the dead."

"Great. Why do I get the creepy job?"

"Some spirits get caught and they can't reach the next world. You can help them to move on. Some won't rest until a wrong has been righted."

"Why me?"

"You inherited it from your grandmother, lovey. She didn't practice publicly but she spoke to me many times about it. She saw her fair share of lost souls. Once you grow into the gift, it will become your new normal – I promise you."

"Well, I'll be keeping the door well and truly shut from now on."

Lynn smiled. "You'll have people around you to help. There will be your protector, who's called the gate-keeper. This will be someone who will always be there for you. They will feel compelled to be at your side and keep evil away."

"Who's that?"

"You won't necessarily know, dear, and neither will they. But you don't get a bridge without a gatekeeper – a bit like you don't get stinging nettles without a dock plant."

"Right, so I'm the spirit world's answer to a bush of stinging nettles?"

Lynn laughed. "That's what I like – great sense of humour. That'll serve you well in this line of work."

I looked up and saw Jeff standing in the doorway. His eyes were wide open.

"Hi, Becky. Do you need a lift home?"

"Thanks, Jeff, but Annie's coming to get me. Thanks for calling for help yesterday. I owe you."

Lynn stood up. "Well I'll be off then."

"What about Zoe and Thomas?" I asked.

"We'll move them on," said Lynn. "Their remains will be moved, of course, and they'll have a funeral but I feel we should do a circle up there, in the woods."

I had no idea what a circle was, but I agreed to join in as Lynn left.

Jeff came over to the bed and passed me a book. *Develop Your Supernatural Power.*

I frowned at him. "Jeff, I'm retiring from my short-lived career as a paranormal detective. I'm opening a café instead."

"Becky, I'm here to protect you. I heard what Lynn said and I'm your gate-keeper." He put a hand to his chest with his hazel eyes wide open. "At your service." He stood to attention. All that was missing was a salute.

Oh my goodness. I was pretty sure Jeff was not my gate-keeper – it probably wasn't even a thing – but I didn't want to upset him.

"Is there anything I can do for you, Becky?"

"Well, you could pop to the hospital café and get me a latte with a caramel shot."

`    ` .   .   .

ANNIE SLOWED the engine as we reached my house. I could see Constance sitting on the wall. I leaned for the car door and regretted it, pains shooting over my battered body.

"Wait a sec," said Annie as she killed the engine. I watched as she ran around the car and opened the door for me.

Constance jumped off the wall and leapt up into my arms and I held her close, her fluffy hair tickled my nose. I squeezed her tight. "Thanks for saving my life, Connie cat."

I looked up at my house, pleased to be home and knowing for sure that I would not be seeing Thomas's shadow in there again.

CHAPTER 20

*O*ver the couple of days I had spent at home convalescing, I decided that I really wanted to push all thoughts of ghosts and the supernatural out of my life. All I wanted was for things to be normal. So as I stood at High Wood, I regretted agreeing to help Lynn with her circle – it was probably the euphoria from the strong painkillers I'd had that led me to thinking it was a great idea.

We stood around the hole where the bodies still lay and a white tent was erected. H said that it would be some time before they were moved but Lynn impressed on us that it was important for their souls to be laid to rest as soon as possible.

As well as Lynn and myself, there was Annie, Izzy and a few of Lynn's friends from the hut. H stood some distance away, overseeing and making sure we did not contaminate the crime scene. Jeff was absent and working his shift at the D.I.Y store. We held hands in a large circle around the area and Lynn called out to Zoe and Thomas, chanting prayers and asking them to move towards the light, to release the chains of pain and hurt, to rest and overcome the worldly death. I stood with my eyes shut but felt an overwhelming need to open them. I saw shining balls of energy dancing before my eyes before lifting and melting into shards of sun which cut through the trees as if Zoe and her father had jumped in an elevator of light. Then all was quiet.

I felt a sense of calm as we headed back through the woods, leaving H there. I wondered what was going through his mind. Annie put her arm in mine as Izzy dodged branches.

"So, what date have you set for opening your café?" said Annie.

IT WAS the day of the café opening – I heaved myself out of bed, I'd been baking well into the early hours. Yes, I could have waited – I needed a proper coffee machine for starters as well as new tables and signage. But I decided that it was better to get on with it and to start making money. After all, it would be summer in a month or so and I needed to gain experience before the school break started. I could invest the profits and decorate the café over the winter months. Lynn had lent me a few tables on a long loan. On the walls, I'd hung pictures of Grandma and historic photographs of the town.

I looked at my watch. I was expecting my new friends. Annie, Izzy, H, Lynn and Jeff had all said they wanted to come over an hour before I opened the doors to the public. Jeff had set me up on various social media sites. He wanted to take pictures and 'go live' on the internet for the opening. Whilst he'd been a little annoying when I'd first met him, he was proving to be extremely helpful and just like the younger brother I never had.

It was soon nine o'clock and I placed menus on the outside tables. On the back of the menu I had printed blurb about Grandma and the charity work she'd done. I'd also managed to find a picture of her winning Branden's Bake-Off, which Izzy had picked up for me from the archives at the Gazette. I looked up to find a woman staring at me from the door.

"Excuse me, are you Becky James?"

"Yes."

"I need you to find out who killed my husband. He drowned."

I looked over to the beach, I'd seen a small crowd over there, a couple of days before with police tape cordoning the area off. I'd heard a man's body had been washed up. *Here we go.* I half expected this, word was bound to get around.

"I'm so sorry, but I don't think I can help you."

"I can see you're busy, but here's my card. Have a think about it and give me a call."

I looked down at the card. On it was the name, 'Mia Hart', with her mobile number.

Mrs Hart walked away. I felt a short buzz up my neck. I slapped my hand on it, as if swatting a fly. *Oh no you don't.*

I popped the card in my apron and returned to laying the tables. The café was going to be named after Grandma as soon as I could afford signage. I looked up and saw Lynn walking along the road, followed by the gang. As they reached me, I noticed that H and Jeff were at the back carrying something large wrapped in paper. *Is it a surfboard?* I groaned. As thoughtful as it was – I didn't want to take up water sports.

"What's that?" I pointed.

"It's your present," said Annie. "From all of us. Izzy said sorry she can't be here, she's seeing the chief editor at the newspaper. He was impressed by the piece she wrote on you."

"Oh, it's good is it?"

"She said she emailed it to you?"

I remembered Izzy had indeed emailed me the draft a few days ago. "I didn't have time to read it with all the baking." I was sure it would be fine. The newspaper was a weekly and she said she would do a two-page spread. *Now that's what I call free advertising.* I was sure she would depict me in a good light, she'd been really complimentary about my cakes.

THE MEDIUM OF BRANDEN BAY | 207

Annie lowered her eyes and bit her lip.

"Well open it then," said Lynn pointing to the huge object.

I ripped off the paper as H held it, smiling at me. I felt a tear come to my eye as I saw it was a brand-new sign, *Connie's Café,* with a picture of a very fluffy ginger cat on it.

Constance meowed and jumped onto the wall, sashaying along. Everyone laughed.

"Oh, my goodness! I don't know what to say."

"We hope you don't mind we changed it from Constance to Connie?" said Lynn.

"Grandma said that that Grandpa used to call her that all the time." I felt a lump in my throat. "Thank you so much."

Constance purred so loudly she could be heard from the wall.

"We wanted to club together to say how glad we are that you moved to Branden Bay and for what you've done for us," said H.

"That's if anyone shows up," I said.

"Oh," said Jeff. "They'll show up alright."

"Why d'you say that?" I asked.

He pulled a copy of the Gazette out of his back pocket and handed it to me. "Izzy's article, of course." I opened it out and on the front was a picture of me on the day of the charity afternoon tea. Above my picture, the headline read:

Local Mystery solved by the Medium of Branden Bay.

"Izzy!" I said looking at the paper in disbelief. "I thought she was just the food critic."

"She was," said Annie. "But after this article she's earned herself a promotion."

"No wonder she kept giving me a grilling."

My new group of friends laughed and patted me on the back. I picked up Constance and ruffled her fluffy head as we all walked into Connie's Café.

THE END

ABOUT THE AUTHOR

As a child Kelly Mason was obsessed with Scooby-Doo, she progressed to reading Edit Blyton, with her favourite series being, The Famous Five. As an adult, she loves Agatha Christie especially her Miss Marple books. And M C Beaton's Agatha Raisin series. Her writing is inspired by the seaside town she lives in, situated on the South West coast of England, and her three sassy cats all of which were strays before she made the mistake of naming them and letting them in the back door!

A note from Kelly.

Thank you very much for reading The Medium of Branden Bay, I hope you continue on to read the next in the series. I loved writing it and inventing the characters. Reviews are really helpful to an author so please leave one if you have a few moments.

If you would like to join my mailing list and receive a digital copy of my free Novella about Becky's Grandma Constance, then please visit

www.kellymasonbooks.com

Books by Kelly Mason:
    Dead Before Midnight
    The Medium of Branden Bay
    The Body in Branden Bay
    The Haunting of Branden Bay

If you want to connect on Facebook you can find me at:
    www.facebook.com/KellyCozyMason

ACKNOWLEDGMENTS

I'd like to thank my creative writing tutor Rosemary Dun who encouraged me to pursue novel writing. Thanks also goes to my mentors Jenny Kane and Alison Knight of Imagine Creative Writing.

I'd also like to thank my best writing friends – Callie Hill, Claire O'Conner and Jenny Taylor, for their support and for sharing the journey with me. And also the friends I met at the Romantic Novelists' Association.

Thanks to my ARC team. And to my Beta readers Cinnomen Matthews McGuigan and Michelle Armitage.

Thanks to my friend Tracey Hadfield who always has a ghost hunting experience to scare me with.

Thanks to my sassy cats, even though they boss me about on a daily basis.

And finally, thanks to my husband Gary who puts up with me tapping away at the keyboard 24/7.

PREVIEW OF THE BODY IN
BRANDEN BAY

Whilst I loved my home by the sea, it was more than a tad spooky. I was scared of ghosts and didn't want to see any more dead people. All I wanted to do was concentrate on the café I had opened in the large front room of my house. I decided I would ignore anything spooky and concentrate on building my café business. To this end, I visited the local bank for help.

"Take a seat, Miss James," said Mr Stone as he looked down his nose at my loan application. "So, you've opened a café on the seafront called." He paused and brought the page closer to his eyes as if he was short-sighted. "Connie's Café?"

"That's right and it's really successful," I said, the enthusiasm oozing from my voice. I shifted in my seat. I guess it was rare for someone in their mid-twenties to own such a large house on the seafront and run a café.

"People love my cakes and I need a professional coffee machine to be able to meet growing demand."

"Hmm, as excited as you are over your recent success, I see you've only been open for – two weeks?" He stared at me and raised his eyebrows as if to say, *you silly girl.*

"Sixteen days, actually."

"And where did your initial investment come from?" He flicked through the pages I'd printed off to support my application.

"I inherited the house and a little money from my Grandmother."

"I see." He shook his head.

"I heard your bank supports small businesses," I pointed to the poster on the wall depicting a suited man handing over a decent-sized wedge of cash to a plumber. I gave him a friendly smile. I knew I'd come to the right place – their adverts were on TV every night.

He frowned. "Indeed. But run before you can walk comes to mind in this case."

"My poor percolator's working overtime. I can't keep up with the filtered coffee orders. It's essential that I invest in a commercial coffee machine to enable me to offer a wide variety of hot drinks, from espresso to latte, to meet the growing demand of my customer base." *Did that sound business-like?* I'd read a similar spiel in the blurb about the coffee machine on-line.

He turned the page. "You're not making any profits."

Oh dear, this guy's hard work. "It's a start up?" I sat up straight and stared him in the eye with what I hoped was an expression dazzling with confidence. When I'd worked in the City of London, I'd dealt with all sorts of people in the hard and fast world of the financial sector. Okay, so I mostly took their coats and poured coffee but still, I was sure I could schmooze this back-water bank manager – or *Assistant Manager,* as I read on his name badge.

I took a deep breath. "The takings are really good, as you can see from the projections I've provided. But my outgoings have been huge. Obvs – I've only just opened." *Whoops! Did I say that last bit out loud?*

"I fear your venture may have novelty value." He gave me a steely glare over the top of his glasses.

"Novelty? It's coffee and cake." I found it hard to keep the sarcasm from my voice and was two cat hairs away from telling him where to stick it.

Talking of cat hairs, I felt movement against my leg which was resting against one of my designer tote bags. Inside was Constance, the stray cat I'd taken in and named after Grandma. Constance followed me every-where and she wriggled again. Worried she might pop out and cause a scene, I leaned down and gently stroked the top of her fluffy-topped ginger head. *Please settle down.*

I felt short bursts of air hit my face as Mr Stone flicked through the final pages of my cobbled-together business plan, far more quickly than he could possibly read it. I sighed. I knew what he was hinting at though, when he'd referred to the café having novelty value. I'd become the subject of local gossip since one of my new friends, Izzy, an ex- model and food critic who was in the process of elevating her career to full-time reporter, did an exclusive on me in the Gazette, hailing me as a paranormal detective after I'd solved a mystery concerning the disappearance of a local girl and her father with the assistance of a shadowy ghost. It was something I was trying to distance myself from and forget. It was down to circumstance rather than any skill on my part that I located their bodies. And I nearly got myself killed in the process. Yes, I saw ghosts, but in no way was I a detective. I was brought back to the present by the sound of Mr Stone's voice.

"I see you have a personal overdraft."

Oh dear. "I'm within my limit."

"And two credit cards."

"Yes that's right." I pulled at the neckline of my top. I'd maxed out on credit buying supplies.

"Leave it with me and we'll review the matter and let you know," he said, pushing my business plan to one side.

I felt it was one of those 'don't-call-us-we'll-call-you' moments that I'd experienced many times when chasing parts in West End shows, armed with my performing arts degree.

"Thanks for your help," I said, picking up my tote bag. Constance poked her fluffy head out and hissed at Mr Stone. He took a sharp intake of breath and his brows knitted together. I quickly slipped out of the bank with my head down.

Once outside, I scolded the mound of ginger fluff in my bag, wagging my finger at her. "Constance, that won't have helped. I'll leave you locked up at home if you carry on like this."

I'd bought Constance a proper pet bag made from a durable material with a neat little window she could look out of. But my feline companion was just as much of a designer diva as her namesake. She'd sniffed her nose at it, sashayed away and got back into Grandma's designer tote bag. But I loved Constance the cat. She felt like family, what with her having the trademark red hair and green eyes which I also possessed.

Feeling someone's gaze upon me, I glanced across the street. I shivered as I saw a man staring at me from the opposite pavement. He had a neat beard and dark hair and wore a business suit. I squinted at him and his gaze caught mine. I felt a pang of sadness in my heart as he looked at me intently. I felt as if he was drawing me in with his stare. I pulled my eyes away. *He's probably someone who'd seen the spread about me in the local rag.* I turned away and pulled my sunglasses down from the top of my head and walked down the sloping High Street towards the seafront. I felt a short burst of static in the nape of my neck and quickly rubbed it away. After a few steps, I glanced over my shoulder to check if the man was still there, but he was gone.

Constance popped her head out of the bag again and meowed at me as if in sympathy.

I sighed. "It seems we're no closer to getting funds for one of those swanky, shiny coffee machines. We'll have to resort to selling instant at this rate." It was embarrassing. "What self-respecting café owner serves up coffee made from granules?"

Constance meowed as though she agreed.

As the promenade came into view, white crests covered the waves as they charged towards the shore. I pulled my coat tight and felt my skirt flapping against my legs. It was mid-June, and a warm one at that, but some days could be blustery with the unpredictable nature of British weather. As I turned onto Beach Road, which ran parallel to the Victorian-style prom, Constance jumped out of the bag and onto the wall, trotting along beside me with her coat ruffling in the wind.

I reached the large terraced Victorian house which had been my home now for a couple of months. The front door was painted a glossy blue. This remained my private entrance. A large bay housed a floor to ceiling window with French doors, which were currently wide open. This was the café entrance. The sign above the door had 'Connie's Café' written on it and a picture of a fluffy ginger puss, just like Constance the cat.

As I entered the café, the hubbub from customers warmed my heart. About half of the tables were filled. Annie, one of my newly-found friends, looked up and I smiled. She was on a week's holiday from work and for some unknown reason had chosen to spend it working with me. She grinned back, her blonde-tinged brown afro matched her brown and gold print dress. She looked as sunny on the outside as she was on the inside. Annie always had a calming influence on me.

"Sorry I'm late back," I said, taking off my jacket and putting on my floral apron. "Business is booming, eh?"

Annie nodded. "I've had a constant stream of customers."

I joined her behind the makeshift counter, which was in fact a table I'd borrowed from a neighbour. "Don't get too excited. I'm not feeling confident after the trip to the bank."

"Did they give you a grilling?" she asked with her eyebrows raised and a hand on her hip.

"The way he treated me, I felt silly for asking. But he said he'd let me know." I looked towards the entrance as the elderly Lady from next door walked in. I called out to her. "Take any seat Mrs Jessup." At least the customers believed in me and were prepared to come in, sit at a hotchpotch of tables and pay cash-only.

"Well, I'm sure the bank will lend you the money. This place is amazing. Everyone's talking about it." Annie was a real cheerleader but I didn't have quite as much confidence as she did after the meeting with Mr Stone.

"Thanks for your help, Annie, I really appreciate it.'

"I wish I could work here instead of the pier."

"Why?"

"Things are tense over there. We had the insurance agent in today – accidents are happening all over the place. Someone is suing them because a tile fell on their head. I might be out of a job at this rate."

"Oh no. As soon as I turn a profit, I'll give you some money to pay for the hours you've done here."

Annie laughed. "No need – I love helping out. The atmosphere is amazing. Honestly it's fun."

I smiled. Annie was a good tonic. I felt the tension I'd picked up in the bank ebb away.

Annie opened her brown eyes and swallowed. "Someone was here looking for you earlier." She turned away to wipe the table top down with a cloth.

"Oh yes?" I said, picking up my pencil and pad. Mrs Jessup looked ready to order.

"A Mia Hart? She said she spoke to you a while ago?"

I remembered the name. "Was it about a cake order?"

Annie looked away scrubbing at the table. "No. It was about your paranormal investigation business." She turned, giving me a guilty smile.

"You know that's not a thing, right?" I placed a hand on my hip. "I hope you told her I can't help with anything paranormal?" So many people had been leaving me their details about ghosts and solving mysteries. Although it wasn't a complete negative as most of them stayed for tea and cake once they'd feasted their eyes on my bakes.

"Mia said she'd already spoken to you. She wants someone to investigate the murder of her husband, Robert. You know, the body in the bay?"

I felt a tingle down my neck. A picture flashed in my mind of a patch on the beach which had been cordoned off with police tape. And a smartly-dressed blonde woman who had approached me on the café opening day. "Oh yes, I remember. But I told her already. I can't help. And I thought the Gazette reported yesterday that the coroner ruled it suicide?"

"Seems his wife disagrees. Poor thing. I know you're not interested in your gift but she was desperate to speak to you. I didn't have the heart to send her away."

Great. I put my hand to the back of my neck as I felt another shock of tell-tale static. *I'm not going down that route again.* "I can't help her – remember? I'm not a psychic detective. That was fake news." I gave a short but nervous laugh as I walked towards Mrs Jessup. I called over my shoulder to Annie. "I just want to concentrate on baking."

Mrs Jessup ordered a pot of tea and a slice of carrot cake. When I reached the kitchen, Annie was already boiling the kettle.

"Mia was desperate to see you," she said.

"But I'm no detective. And there's no missing body in this case. We know where his body is. The newspaper said it's been released and the memorial service is planned for next week."

"True, but I felt awful for her. So I said you'd call back to let her know whether it was a yes or no." Annie handed me an order slip, upon which she'd scribbled Mia's number.

I shook my head. "I'll call her this evening. But it's definitely no." I placed the paper in the pocket of my apron and glanced at the clock. It was twelve already and the lunch time rush would start soon.

I took Mrs Jessup's small pot of tea out of the kitchen and into the main café, placing it at her table and fetched her cake.

The sea breeze blew my hair as I rearranged the chairs around the outside café-style tables, in case any customers wanted to brave a blustery alfresco lunch. Constance perched herself on the wall touting for strokes from passers-by. She hissed and I peered over to the prom as static shot up my back. The suited guy I'd seen earlier in the High Street was across the road, leaning against the sea wall.

To read more see Amazon Store:

Kelly Mason. The Body in Brandon Bay

Printed in Great Britain
by Amazon

42160151R00131